SHEM

Book 3

From the Trilogy

HEROES OF OLD

Chapter 1

After Noah was 500 years old, he became the father of Shem, Ham, and Japheth. - Genesis 5:32

Shem held his breath, raised a boulder with both hands above his head, and slammed it down onto the top of the fence post. The post lowered slightly.

"Finally!"

He let the boulder fall to the ground next to his feet and stepped back to survey his work. Salty sweat ran down his face and stung his eyes. Clad only in loincloth and sandals, he tossed his head briskly to one side, letting the perspiration fly off his long hair like a dog after coming out of the water. He wiped across his eyes with a small cloth tied around one of his wrists, and then looked down the row of new posts extending from the sheep pen to the corner post of the older fence.

"We almost set them in a straight line," he proclaimed.

Rounding the corner of the sheep pen, Japheth staggered toward him with an armload of newly cut branches. He opened his arms and dropped the load next to the posts. "Whew! We should have this repaired by sundown."

Shem leered over his shoulder in the direction of his youngest brother's dwelling. "We would be finished now, if Ham were here."

Japheth handed him the end of one of the branches. "I am sure he has a good reason for not showing up."

Shem shook his head. "Ham is too comfortable being the youngest. We have always helped him and pulled him along. He does not think about returning the favors."

He took the end of the branch and tied it to a post as Japheth secured the other end to the post next to him. Japheth handed him another branch and they tied off the next rail.

As they continued to add rails to the fence, Japheth asked, "Do you really think someone other than the sheep broke the old fence down?"

"I am certain of it," Shem said. "I inspected the area and found sandal prints around the broken-down area. The sheep did not just run away. They were carried."

"Who would do this?"

Shem repositioned himself near the next post. "I believe our father is at the root of this."

"Our father?" Japheth stood and faced Shem. "He would never do anything like this. How could you say that?"

Shem smiled. He enjoyed teasing his little brother. It took so little to get him riled. He picked up another rail and extended it to Japheth. Japheth made no move to grab it.

Shem continued holding the rail out. "I did not say father did this. I think it was done because of one of his confrontations." He shook the end of the rail and motioned with his eyes for Japheth to take it.

Japheth locked eyes with him, paused, and then took the rail. "Who did father confront this time?"

"Bardo."

"Not Bardo," Japheth rolled his eyes. "Father did not go after him?"

"Like a bear to a bee hive." Shem lashed his end of the rail to the post. "I think his sons did this to send Father a message."

Japheth shook his head. "Why does he do that?"

"You know Father." Shem shrugged. "He thinks he is Yahweh's moral voice to his people."

Japheth dropped his end of the rail and threw up his hands. "All the people do is laugh at him."

"And us." Shem added. "We are the only ones who heed his words."

Japheth laughed. "That is because he is still stronger than the two of us put together."

"And that is why my fence is broken and not Father's." Shem motioned to the rail end Japheth dropped. "Talk while you work, or we will never get this–"

"Shem…Shem!" A shrill cry came from the other side of the sheep pen.

Shem stood and turned his ear to the sound. "That sounds like Jazel."

A second voice cried out. "Japheth!"

"Temani?" Japheth's head jerked up. "Sounds like trouble."

Shem grabbed his tunic off one of the posts and pulled it over his head. He and his brother ran toward the shouts of their wives. Upon reaching the sheep pens, they found the women with head scarves down around their shoulders, tear smeared cheeks, and out of breath.

Both women burst into rapid speech, making no sense to Shem. His wife, Jazel, grabbed his arm and tried pulling him back along the path from which they came.

Shem took her by her shoulders. "Hold on." He looked into her dark puffy eyes. "Tell me slowly. What is wrong?"

"Hurry!" she cried. "Your father has lost his mind!"

Shem continued to stare, not understanding her outburst. "What do you mean?"

Temani pulled on Japheth's tunic. "Your father is sobbing uncontrollably. He keeps crying out something about Yahweh's judgment, and that everyone is going to die."

Chills went down Shem's spine. He caught Japheth's eyes. "No, it cannot be."

Japheth took his wife's hand from his tunic. "Temani, where is Father?"

Temani looked toward their father's dwelling and took a breath. "He is home."

"And Mother?"

"She is with him."

"Come," Shem said. "Let us hurry before Father tears the house down."

The four of them quickened their pace up the path toward their parent's home.

***

When they reached the dwelling, the front door stood wide open.

Both brothers called out, "Father...Mother!"

Shem and Japheth entered and looked around. A stool, tipped on its side, lay next to the eating table. A wooden plate, spoon, and cup lie in a mixture of cooked vegetables strewn across the floor.

Shem shook his head. *Father is angry.*

From the sleeping room, Japheth called out. "They are gone. Should we check the wood shop?"

Shem checked behind the door. "Do not bother. Both their walking staffs are gone."

Japheth started for the door. "They must be headed for the ledge."

"Jazel," Shem called out as he followed after his brother. "You and Temani go find Ham and Gaddi. Tell them to meet us at the ledge."

The two women hurried off one way and the brothers another. After crossing a field scattered with young sprouts of various vegetables, the men came to a well-worn path that ascended past a layer of scrub brush and then disappeared into the thick foliage up the side of a hill.

Japheth inspected the ground near the scrub brush. "They definitely are at the ledge."

"I wonder," Shem spoke more to himself than to his brother. "Why does he like to sit and gaze over the village, when everyone there ignores his efforts to reform them?"

Japheth shrugged and continued up the path. The path zig zagged into the woods ascending higher and higher, finally stopping at a clearing near the edge of a solid rock cliff.

Off to the side, on a small wood-hewed bench, sat their mother and father, arm in arm, her head resting on his shoulder. Both quietly gazed across the valley.

Shem and Japheth slowly approached from behind.

"Father...Mother," Shem asked softly. "Are you well?"

Their mother raised her head and wiped tears from her face. "We are fine."

Shem stepped around the bench to face them. His father continued to stare with tear-filled eyes at the scene below. Shem followed his gaze. Looking beyond his family's four dwellings, each with their fertile plot of land nestled next to the forest. Past the stream that meandered through various plots of farmland, lay the village. Ant-like villagers going about their daily chores moved in the streets.

"Father," Shem whispered. "What is wrong?"

His father slowly turned his eyes toward Shem. *"We are wrong, son. We are wrong."*

"What do you mean, Father?"

Noah looked at Japheth and then back to Shem. "Go get Ham and your wives and I will explain."

Shem looked past his father at Ham, who just entered the clearing from the woods. Gaddi, Jazel, and Temani followed close behind. Ham made eye contact. Shem glared back, letting him know of his anger for not helping with the fence.

Shem motioned to his father. "We are all here now."

Ham, pulling Gaddi behind him, came and stood next to Japheth. Temani and Jazel joined their husbands. Their mother stayed on the bench.

Noah raised himself from the bench to his full stature and briefly glanced upward. He wiped his eyes with his sleeve and cleared his throat.

"Yahweh has spoken to me."

Shem cringed inside and held Jazel tightly as he waited for his father to speak. *What Temani had said back at the sheep pen could not be what Father said.*

His mind flashed back to the dream that his grandfather had shared with them when they were children. *Yahweh would not really allow everyone to die, would he?*

Chapter 2

Noah raised an arm and pointed out over the valley. "Look down on the village where you have lived your whole lives. Who has not experienced harm from the evil deeds of the people in our village?"

While his father paused, countless confrontations with the villagers came to Shem's mind. Life had not been easy for he and his brothers. Having a father that, claimed not only to speak with Yahweh, but insisted that they live according to the old ways, made him a target for ridicule and physical abuse amongst his peers. How many fights had he and his brothers been lured into standing up for his father's convictions?

His father continued. "Violence has become a way of life. Seeking sensual pleasures are sought above moral commitments. Instead of obedience to Yahweh, every family relies on their personal idols to bestow upon them false righteousness.

"And it is not only the people of our village. The people of every other village on earth act the same."

His father shook his head. "Yahweh is grieved over those he created...and has decided to put an end to them."

A collective gasp escaped from the mouths of Shem and his family.

Ham fidgeted. "You cannot mean that, Father? Yahweh is surely not going to kill everyone. What kind of a God does that?"

Noah lowered his eyebrows and puffed out his chest. "A *righteous* God would do that. A God who is so pure that no evil can, or should, stand before him. That is what kind of God would do that."

Ham shrugged and looked away.

"Yahweh is righteous," Noah continued in a little softer voice. "But he is also a loving God. Our conduct has found favor with him and he has decided to save our family from this judgment. I have already told your mother. Now I will tell you what Yahweh has decreed." He motioned with his arms. "Sit."

Shem, his brothers, and their wives, all sat.

"Yahweh is going to bring floodwaters upon the earth to wipe out all mankind under heaven. He wants us to build an ark to float upon these waters. An ark large enough to hold the eight of us and two of every animal upon the earth."

Shem and his brothers looked at each other. He heard Ham mumbling under his breath.

Their father continued. "The ark will be three hundred cubits long, fifty cubits wide, and thirty cubits tall with three levels inside."

"Three hundred cubits!" Japheth laughed. "You have a woodshop, but we have never built anything so large. It will be impossible."

Shem nodded in agreement.

Ham spoke up. "And how are we going to find and catch all these animals?"

Noah frowned and shook his head again. "You ask these questions because you do not know Yahweh. I do not yet know the answers to your questions, but I am sure he will give us the ability to do all that is necessary. Yahweh will provide."

Shem could no longer look at his father. *Jazel was right. Father really has lost his mind. What are we to do with this nonsense he is speaking? How could any of this be true?*

Shem got lost in his thoughts.

"Shem."

"Eh…What?"

Ham chuckled behind him.

"We will need your oxen to haul timber," he said. "You and your brothers will need to build a pen for them at the edge of the woods to save time bringing them all the way from your dwelling each day."

Confused, Shem stammered, "Ye-Yes, Father."

"Ham," Noah said. "You will need to fire up your forge for more metal saw blades and spikes for securing beams together."

Ham answered. "Yes, Father."

"Japheth, we will need all the beeswax from your hives to mix with tree sap and tar to make pitch to coat the wood on the ark."

Japheth answered as his brothers did, "Yes, Father."

Shem knew his brothers. They agreed with Father as he did, but he doubted they believed what they heard. *I will meet with them later and discuss how to approach father's craziness.*

Noah turned his back and looked across the valley. "I have shed many tears for these people. My sons, go to your homes now and console your wives. We have no family to lose but your aging grandfather. I will speak with him about this matter later today. I know he has waited a long time for this day and is trusting Yahweh for his future, but each of your wives will suffer the loss of father, mother, brothers, sisters, and much more. Go and weep with them."

Shem watched his father go back to the bench and sit next to his mother. Once again Henna laid her head on his shoulder and both gazed out across the valley. Shem, his brothers, and their wives looked at each other. Tears streaked the cheeks of the women.

Finally, Shem rose and pulled Jazel up by her hand. "Come. Let us return home."

His brothers and their wives followed silently behind them. Only whispers were heard on the path back down.

***

Back in their dwelling, Shem and Jazel sat across from each other at the eating table. Shem could not ignore the worry in his wife's eyes. He had always been able to lose himself in those deep, dark eyes. But now, they cried out for some words of reassurance.

Shem spoke to those eyes. "Father is from the men of old. He is tired and confused. All his life he has confronted these people and been ridiculed for his effort. I think he has given up and has conjured up in his mind a way of shedding his burden for them. Do not worry your heart over his words."

Jazel stared back, tears forming in her eyes. "Do not be angry with me for speaking so, but are you not avoiding your own thoughts about your grandfather's dream? Did you not tell me earlier in our marriage that your grandfather, Lamech, had a recurring dream about this very thing? Did he not make you and your brothers memorize this dream? Are you not thinking about it? It is the first thing that came to my mind as your father spoke to us."

Shem rose from his stool and began pacing. In a way, he wished he had never shared his grandfather's dream with her. She was right. He was avoiding it. He did not want it to be true.

"It was just a child's tale, told by an old man."

"An old man?" Jazel half-laughed. "Did he not tell this same dream to your father when your father was a child? Was he an old man then?"

Shem knew he was losing this battle. One of Jazel's traits he loved was her ability to think through problems. But now, it was working against him.

"It cannot be true." Shem threw his hands up. "How could my grandfather know about this so long ago?"

Jazel rose from her stool and walked over to her husband. She placed her soft hands against his cheeks and kissed him. "I think you are afraid to believe."

Shem closed his eyes and hugged her. *Afraid? Maybe I am afraid.*

He released her and sat on the stool again. "What should I do? I do not know what to believe."

Jazel went into the food preparation room and began selecting vegetables to cook for dinner.

"I think," she called out, "that you should eat a good meal, get a long night's rest, and in the morning, go talk to your grandfather about his dream."

Shem sat in silence reflecting on the dream. Jazel brought out a loaf of bread and placed it in front of him. Before she could pull her hand back, he grabbed it and pulled her into his lap and nuzzled her neck.

"I will go see Grandfather." He paused between kisses. "As long as you come with me."

She giggled. "I will go, but right now, I have a meal to prepare."

He continued nuzzling. "And I have a wife to show my appreciation to."

When Shem finally closed his eyes in bed, he felt a resolve to seek the truth about his grandfather's dream and his father's *so-called* revelation from Yahweh.

I do not know Yahweh as father does. I do not know what he might do. I have always relied on Father to tell me. Maybe I need to change that.

Chapter 3

Shem rose early and finished securing the rails on the fence while it was still cool. Returning inside, he waited as Jazel packed a small pouch with a few dates, nuts and part of a loaf of bread. Shem grabbed his cloak off the peg by the door. Jazel threw her shawl over her head, and the two of them set out to his grandfather's dwelling on the other side of the village.

With the village in view, Shem pointed to a path leading off to one side. "My parents used to walk us on a path around the edge of the village to reach Grandfather's dwelling. They felt the marketplace and some of the behaviors that have become normal for this area were not good for us to experience."

"My parents," Jazel said, "would leave us at home when they went to the village, and not return until after we were all asleep. I shudder to think what they did for all that time."

Shem put an arm around her back. "Today, I do not want to take the time to go around, so stay close."

The nearer they ventured to the village center, the dwellings on both sides of the street no longer had spaces between them. Block and plaster had long ago replaced the older wood dwellings. Crates and tables lined each side of the street, bearing various fruits, vegetables, herbs and spices for sale. Ornate pots, eating utensils and scarves hung from cords strung above the tables.

Crowds milled through the market. Chatter between the merchants and buyers almost seemed melodic. Shem and Jazel took in all the sights, sounds, and aromas. Jazel reached out and felt all the colorful fabrics she passed.

Shem noticed in one area, several women with braided hair, dangly jewelry, and wearing almost nothing, beckoning men that strolled close to come with them through a dark doorway behind them. Several men loitered nearby, haggling over prices. One of the men looked a lot like the older son of Bardo. Shem urged Jazel on.

Jazel pulled her shawl tight over her head. "I would hate to think what this area is like after dark."

Shem pressed on, leading Jazel around several people staggering toward them. Twice, Jazel almost tripped over others sleeping in the narrow street.

Sweet smoke and stale wine thickened the air around him. They quickened their pace, and soon, all sights and sounds were finally behind them.

The number of dwellings grew sparse, giving way to fields, some sprouting new growth, some with sheep and goats calling to them from the opposite side of fences. Soon, the pathway split and they took the one heading toward the stream. Crossing a small bridge, they came to an old, run down dwelling looking like the woods were slowly enveloping it.

Stepping up onto the porch, Shem called out, "Grandfather, it is Shem, son of Noah."

He waited, but heard no movement inside. He shouted a little louder, "Grandfather, it is Shem, son of Noah."

Still no sound from inside.

Shem took Jazel's hand. "Let us go around back. Grandfather spends a lot of time talking to Grandmother back there."

"I thought your grandmother died a long time ago."

"She did."

Shem led Jazel down a well-worn path to a spot of flowers surrounding a large flat, bluish stone rising out of the ground about to the height of their knees. A small bench facing the stone sat empty.

Shem rested his hand on the top of the stone.

"This stone used to lie as the hearth inside next to their fire pit. My grandmother, Elidia, loved to sit on it in the evenings and listen to exciting tales shared by family and travelers. Grandfather removed this from the fire pit and placed it and these flowers over the place she is buried."

Jazel smiled. "From what I heard," she said, "Elidia had tales of her own adventures to share."

Shem took Jazel's hand and started back up the path toward the dwelling. "Yes, Grandmother's abduction by men bent on harming the First Man is the initial reason he went north. After she was rescued, they continued north where he met the First Man. Grandfather married her before they returned home. It was quite an adventure for both of them."

Jazel squeezed his arm. "You have never told me about what happened between your grandfather and the First Man."

Shem shrugged. "I think it would be better if my grandfather told you."

They made their way to the back door. He pounded on it with his fists. "Grandfather, wake up and let us in."

Still no response.

Shem opened the door. The two of them stepped inside.

"It smells musty," Jazel said.

Shem nodded. "None of the windows are open. Did not your father say he was coming here yesterday?"

Shem surveyed the room. "Yes, just before we left the ledge."

They walked through the food preparation room and into the eating area.

Jazel stopped at the table. "Everything is neat and in its place." She ran her hand across the table. "And clean."

Shem walked across to the sleeping room and opened the door a crack. "The whole inside has been cleaned and tidied. I wonder if he went..."

Jazel scooted up behind Shem. "What is it?"

Shem swung the door open the rest of the way. "He did not go on a journey."

Jazel peeked her head around Shem. "Oh my!"

His grandfather was lying on his side on a bed of skins. Half curled, with a faint smile etched across his face. He hugged an extra tunic close to his head.

Shem stared at his face. "I do not think he is sleeping."

Jazel stepped closer. "Oh, no."

Shem placed his hand to his grandfather's pale forehead. "Cold as the stream."

Jazel put her hand on Shem's shoulder. "Oh, Shem. I am sorry."

Shem softly touched the fabric of the extra tunic. "This was Grandmother's tunic he is holding." He slowly pulled the blanket over his grandfather's head. After Father left, he probably spent half the night cleaning."

"What do we do now?" Jazel asked.

"When we get home, I will tell Father. I and my brothers will come back and bury him next to Grandmother."

"What is this over here?" Jazel inspected a large wooden wash tub sitting on the floor at the foot of the bed filled to the top with water. Floating on the water was a wooden bowl filled with acorns.

Shem bent down, picked up the bowl, and studied the contents. Under the acorns he found a clear quartz crystal stone. He counted the acorns.

"Eight acorns," he whispered to himself.

Jazel put her hand out and received the bowl from him. "What does that mean?"

Shem looked back at the bed with his grandfather and then sat down on the corner of the bed. "I think he put this together to represent his dream."

Jazel sat next to him. "The dream he made you and your brothers memorize?"

"Yes. The water in the tub must represent the rising waters in his dream."

He picked the quartz crystal from the acorns. "This crystal represents the jewel he was given by the First Man. When the waters rose, he placed the jewel in a bowl with eight seeds. The bowl floated on top of the rising waters a long time before the waters resided and it came to rest on dry ground. The jewel broke into eight pieces and each piece joined with a seed. The seeds were planted in the new soil and forest grew from them, each with a bit of the jewel among them."

"What do the acorns mean?" Jazel asked.

Shem shook his head and smiled. "The acorns are us." He picked one and gave it to her. "That one is you." He picked up another. "This one is me." He held it next to his face. "Do you see the resemblance?"

"I see that you are a nut."

Shem ignored her. "The other six acorns must be Father and Mother, Japheth and Temani, and Ham and Gaddi."

"And the bowl," Jazel proclaimed, "represents the ark that your father wants you to build."

Shem stared at the bowl in Jazel's hand. "The ark?"

Shem did not want to say it, but the conclusion was inescapable. He took the bowl and held it high. "Yes, the bowl is the ark *we* are going to build."

Chapter 4

Because of his father's presence during the burial of Shem's grandfather the prior day, Shem had no opportunity to speak privately with his brothers. Today, his father's *revelation* still echoed loudly in his mind as he approached Ham's dwelling. Did his grandfather's dream and his father's revelation both come from Yahweh? They both couldn't have imagined it.

Black smoke rose from behind the small home.

Clang…clang…clang…clang.

He must be at his forge.

Shem walked around to the back and found his brother under a roofed framework. Stripped to the waist, he hammered on a heavy metal rod. Near him, out of an opening in a domed brick oven, white flames threw off an eerie glow that glistened off Ham's sweaty muscular frame.

Ham turned the rod and hit it with his hammer.

Clang!

He turned it again and hit it again.

Clang!

"Ham," Shem yelled.

Ham looked up, smirked, and doused the glowing end of the rod into a tub of water. He tossed his hammer onto a small wooden table covered with burn marks and searched for something on a metal rack.

"What are you doing here? I thought you were erecting a shelter for your oxen today."

Shem fingered a of couple metal tools hanging from the rack. "The shelter can wait another day. I see you have not started forging new saw blades yet."

Ham put his hands on his hips. "Did you come here to check on me for Father?"

Shem put both palms out toward his brother. "No, but Father is what I want to talk about."

Ham laughed as he grabbed a cloth and wiped the sweat from his face. "You want to know if I believed what Father said."

Shem looked for a place to sit, stalling until he could get his embarrassment under control. He up-righted a weathered stool lying nearby, sat, and leaned his back against the wall of the structure.

"Well, do you?" Shem asked.

Ham smirked again. "Of course not."

He sat on the rim of the water tub and leaned forward. "I know Father has always spoken to everyone about what Yahweh tells him. Most of those who know him make jokes about how he walks with Yahweh. You, Japheth, and I have defended him most of our lives."

"But what about the dream?" Shem asked.

"The dream?" Ham stood. "Is that why you are here? What is wrong with you? The dream was just a dream. Our grandfather may have believed it and he may have made us believe it. Young children believe everything their parents tell them. But, when we grow older, we realize our parents, or grandparents, do not know everything."

Shem rubbed the back of his neck. "Did you see the bowl with the eight acorns floating in the tub? Eight acorns. There are eight of us."

"Eight of us?" Ham raised his voice. "It will take many seasons to build a boat as big as father wants. How many of us will there be next harvest, or the harvests after that when our wives bear children? In two or three seasons there could be eleven of us."

Shem looked down. He had been wanting children for some time.

Ham bent down and shook the tub of water causing rings of ripples to converge in the center.

"Shem. Look at this water. We both know how much water it would take to float a boat as large as he wants us to make. Where is this water going to come from? Do you think it is just going to fall out of the sky?"

Shem stood and looked his brother in the eyes. "What are you going to do with Father? You cannot ignore or disobey him."

Ham picked up the rod from within the water tub and placed it into the fire. "I will make new saw blades for him and wait for him to forget about this."

Shem stared at the fire. "You may be waiting a long time."

***

Shem's parents' dwelling lay between Ham's and Japheth's dwelling. Not yet ready to face his father before speaking with Japheth, Shem decided to walk through the fields around the edge of their property to bypass any chance of running into him.

Ham's questions ran through his mind as he maneuvered carefully across rows of newly sprouted beets. *Where is the water going to come from to float the ark? And, not only to float it, but to float it far above the hill on which they had looked across the valley.*

Maybe he was right. I was so sure when we found Grandfather's acorns in the bowl.

"Son!"

"Huh!" Shem jerked, cut his stride short and trampled a beet sprout.

"Watch the beets," Noah barked.

"Father," Shem stammered. "I did not see you."

Noah laughed. "You must have a lot on your mind. But I am glad to see you out here looking to see where we are going to build this ark."

"I...uh, yes." Shem took a breath and looked toward the woods. "I need to put the shelter for my oxen someplace close."

His father's eyes sparked an eagerness to his face. He pointed toward a field where his goats grazed. "We will move my goats to your field to graze with your sheep. See there, where those beets stop and the grazing field starts," he pointed to the end of the rows of beets. "That is where we will put the front of the ark. Then measure three hundred cubits toward our dwelling, over there," he pointed toward his dwelling. "And that, close to home, will be the other end. What do you think?"

Shem's head swirled. "I...uh...think that is a good place."

Noah turned and looked toward the woods. "I think you should build your shelter over there some place."

Shem followed his gaze. "Yes, I will begin moving the lumber tomorrow."

"Son." His father put his hand on Shem's shoulder. "Your faith is strong. It makes me happy to see you ready to do Yahweh's will. I hope my other sons are as faithful as you."

Shem feigned a smile as he backed away a couple steps. "Thank you, Father. I...ah, will go see how Japheth is doing with his...uh...faith."

Shem turned and headed for Japheth's.

His father called after him. "Get him to help you with the shelter."

Shem did not turn to reply but raised one hand high in acknowledgement and kept on walking.

Seems like Father has put his grieving behind him. It looks like he is enjoying this.

What am I going to say to Japheth?

***

As Shem neared Japheth's dwelling, a sweet aroma filled his senses. Groves of fruit trees almost surrounded their home–apples, pears, peaches, and his favorite, cherries. Birds flittered everywhere and filled the air with music.

Shem inhaled deeply before stepping up onto the porch. Even with all the different aromas outside, he could smell hot apple pie wafting through the open window next to the door. His mouth salivated.

"Japheth," he called out. "It is Shem."

He heard a pitter-patter of small footsteps and then the door opened a crack. A pair of small eyes peaked through the opening about waist high.

Shem bent down to eye level. "Who are you?"

The door shut and a pitter-patter was followed by normal footsteps.

Temani opened the door. She wore an apron over her tunic and had a white flour smudge on one of her cheeks and another on her forehead running up into her hair.

"Shem. I am sorry. I did not hear you." She wiped her hand with a cloth. "My sister, Galal, and her daughter, are helping me with my baking. Japheth is out back with his bees."

"Thanks. I will go around." Shem stepped off the porch. "Whatever is on the other side of that door sure smells good."

Temani waved. "I will send a pie over to Jazel later this evening."

Shem walked around to the back, making his way through a small grove of apple trees. Just past the grove, in an open grassy area, stood four rows of crate-like wooden boxes, about ten in each row. The boxes sat on small platforms, two per platform. Bees swarmed all around them.

Shem spotted Japheth at the far end of the rows doing something at a vacant platform. A small column of smoke rose from a fire pit just beyond him. Shem kept his distance, circling the area to reach Japheth from the other direction.

Japheth looked up and waved to him. "Come closer."

Shem moved a couple steps nearer.

Japheth motioned with his hand. "Closer. They will not sting you if you stay in the smoke."

Shem looked at the smoke, then at the bees and slowly crept up next to his brother and whispered, "What are you doing?"

"You do not need to whisper. Our voices will not alarm the bees."

Shem continued to glance nervously at the bees on the other platforms as he peered around his brother. Japheth had some sort of fruit mixture on a wooden slab in front of him.

"I am crushing apples and pears into a sweet, juicy nectar. I will put this slab with the nectar next to the hives. The bees drink the juice and keep close to their hives. I am almost finished."

Shem could not keep his eyes off the bees circling around them. Several landed on the platform and were helping themselves to a meal.

Shem started backing away. "I will wait for you over there." He gestured toward a table and stools nearer the dwelling.

Japheth grinned and shook his head. He finished mashing and mixing the fruit mixture. He then placed the platform with the mixture near the center row of hives and joined Shem.

"I am glad you came," Japheth said. "I wanted to talk to you about what Father said."

Shem leaned his forearms on the table. "Go ahead. I am listening."

"What Father spoke reminded me of Grandfather's dream. We all enjoyed listening to Grandfather tell us his dream over and over again. It amused me as a child. Now it frightens me."

Shem nodded.

Japheth lowered his voice. "What Father claims seems to verify that Grandfather's dream was from Yahweh, and that we will be involved with the fulfillment. I do not know what to think. Temani is worried sick." Japheth's eyes surveyed the open window near them. "She wants her family to come with us on the ark."

Shem stood quickly and pulled his brother by the arm a few steps away from the dwelling. "You have not told her family about it, have you?"

Japheth shook his head. "We have not told anyone. They would think we were crazy. What are we to do?"

Shem massaged his chin. "I have to admit, the dream, although ages ago, fits into what Father said. But, a boat three hundred cubits long, built on Father's land? Where is all the water going to come from to float it? There is not enough water in all the land to fulfill what the dream speaks of."

"You do not believe Father?"

"I believe Father thinks he heard from Yahweh. But, for all we know, he might have dreamt it the same as Grandfather."

Japheth stood. "Father is closer to Yahweh than anyone else we know. He has never deceived us. If he says Yahweh is going to bring enough water to float an ark, Yahweh will make a way to do it."

Shem raised his hands between he and his brother. "I did not say it could not happen. I only meant it would take a miracle."

"It already is a miracle."

Shem blinked before he spoke. "What do you mean?"

"I mean, Mother and Father lived for ages without having children. And then in a few short seasons, they bore the three of us. It should have been long enough for them to have given birth to twenty or thirty. But it is just us three."

"So?"

"So, we know that in Grandfather's dream eight seeds float over judgment. Grandfather told us the seeds in the bowl were his seeds, his descendants. He had the dream before he even had any wife or children. Father has told us before that he is the only child of our grandfather left alive that he is aware of. This is probably the only time ever that Grandfather's seeds will total eight.

"The three of us have been married long enough to have had many children, but Yahweh has miraculously kept us without. We eight are the only ones who *can* fulfill Grandfather's dream."

Shem sat dumbfounded. He marveled at Japheth's faith. Feelings of shame welled up within him. He saw the dream represented in Grandfather's water tub and believed but had allowed Ham's doubts to snatch it away. His grandfather felt the dream so important, it was the last thing he communicated to them before he died.

I am such a fool.

"Shem." Japheth stared at him.

"Sorry...I...You are right about the dream."

Japheth smiled.

Shem looked back toward his dwelling. "I…ah…came here to ask if you can help me erect a shelter for my oxen tomorrow at the edge of Father's fields. He wants to start building as soon as possible."

Japheth stood. "Sure. I will come by after breakfast."

"Thanks." Shem turned to leave. "I will begin moving the wood to the location."

"But you have not answered my original question," Japheth said. "What are we going to do?"

Shem turned his palms up. "We are going to build an ark…and expect another miracle."

Shem headed home with various emotions warring in his heart. He was embarrassed by Japheth's unwavering faith, and angry, at himself, for letting Ham, of all people, sway his judgment. Deeper down, though, a question begged to be answered.

Am I foolish for believing in miracles?

Chapter 5

Japheth handed a wooden pole up to Shem. "This is the last one."

"Good." Shem steadied himself on the roof and secured the pole along the edge. He then stood and surveyed their work from the roof.

"All that is left is a little straw for the floor and tomorrow I will bring my two oxen to their new home."

"Feed them well," Japheth said. "They will need all their strength for what comes next."

From atop the roof, Shem spotted two men approaching from the edge of the woods. "Hmm, looks like trouble coming."

Japheth stepped around to the side and faced the woods. "Can you tell who they are?"

"They walk like Bardo's sons, Arad and Koz."

Japheth smirked. "They cannot stand not knowing everybody else's business."

Shem stepped down from the roof to the top of the railing, and then jumped to the ground. "They want to see if there is anything here they can profit from."

Japheth moved and stood next to his brother facing the approaching men.

The two men wore heavy cloaks over their tunics. Large knife blades gleamed from below their belts. They ignored Shem and Japheth, stepping past them with no verbal greeting and began inspecting the newly built shelter.

Arad scratched his unkempt beard and shook one of the railings. "What is this supposed to be?"

Shem put his hand on the rail to steady it. "I will keep my oxen here while we haul timber from the woods."

"Timber?" Koz said, rubbing a paled scar slanting across his right cheek. "What are you building way over here?"

Shem made eye contact with Japheth.

"We are building…" Japheth volunteered, "a structure to hold more animals."

Shem smiled at his brother.

"More animals?" Arad still looked at the shelter. "I heard you lost some of your animals a while back. Broke out of your sheep pen."

Shem's stomach tightened with anger. "A couple. We are looking to get a few more from outside the valley."

Arad shook the rail again. "I see you are building your rails stronger now. You should not lose any more with these."

"We have not seen your father for a while," Koz said as the two men turned to leave. "Not since you lost your sheep. Is he well?"

Shem knew they were just making sure that the message of knocking down his sheep fence was understood. "He is well, but I do not think you will be seeing him much for a while. He is helping us haul timber and build."

The men nodded and, as they walked away, Koz called over his shoulder, "We will miss our confrontations with him."

Japheth spoke under his breath. "And soon, we will miss our confrontations with you."

Shem smiled. "You still have your sense of humor. Go home to Temani. Thanks for helping me today."

He watched Japheth go and then gathered a few of his tools and headed home also.

It would be nice not to have any more of these confrontations with the Bardo brothers anymore.

***

The next morning Shem scattered straw on the ground inside the shelter and led his two oxen through the gate.

He patted the hindquarters of the second ox as it entered. "Relax in your new home while you can. Soon you two will be working hard."

Shem decided to walk to the location his father pointed out for building the ark.

At least the field is used for grazing and not planting. It is hard and flat. But, how are we going to build something so big?

Shem caught movement out of the corner of his eye. Turning, he saw Jazel waving to him from the edge of the field. She was coming from the direction of their dwelling.

What does she want?

She waited at the edge of the field until he got closer and then called to him. "Your father has asked us all to come to his home."

Shem shook his head. "What has Yahweh told him now?"

Jazel grabbed his arm in hers. "Now, do not be like that."

They walked together to his parent's dwelling. Both Japheth and Ham were already seated in the eating room chatting. Jazel went into the food-preparation room to join Temani and Gaddi helping their mother-in-law prepare the meal.

Shem pulled a stool from under the table and sat next to Japheth, across from Ham. His father was nowhere to be seen.

"Where is Father?"

Ham pointed to the back door. "He is out in his woodshop. He told us to wait inside."

Shem called out to his mother. "Mother, shall I go out and get him?"

She called back. "No, I hear him coming in now."

The back door opened, but no one entered. A large object wrapped in a cloak held up by two hands slowly squeezed through the doorway. Then, their father emerged behind the object.

Japheth jumped up to help his father.

"I can carry it," Noah spouted. "But, you could close the door."

Shem and Ham stood as their father, bundle in arms, approached the table, followed closely by the women. His eyes sparkled. He carefully set the bundle on the table. They watched their father slowly align it with the table sides. He stood briefly and scanned the wide-eyed faces around the table.

"Father," Japheth pleaded, "What is it?"

Noah quickly removed the cloak and stepped back.

Shem stared, but could not speak. There, on the table in front of him, sat a rectangular box-like structure reaching almost the length of the table, but only a fourth as wide and high. Tiny window openings lined the object near the top. A small door hung open on one side, hinging across the bottom, creating a ramp for entry. Other than that, there were no other openings.

Their father puffed up his chest and announced, "This is what we are going to build."

"The...ark?" Shem could hardly get the word through his lips.

"Father!" Japheth's face broke a wide smile. "You made this in your shop?"

Noah's face beamed. "According to Yahweh's instructions."

Shem glanced at Ham, who remained silent.

"Of course," his father said. "The outside will be covered with pitch to keep the water out, and the inside will have three levels, but this is the ark that will carry us and the animals over the water."

"When do we begin?" Japheth asked.

His father looked at Shem. "Are your oxen in their new shelter?"

"I moved them this morning," Shem said.

"Then bring your axes, saws, and ropes. Tomorrow we begin hauling timber."

Henna pushed her way past Shem with a large plate of steaming potatoes. "Tomorrow can wait," she said as she set the plate next to the ark. She motioned to her husband. "Now get your plaything off the table so we can eat."

Noah hesitated, lowered his brows, and then pulled the ark to his side of the table. Henna, with hands on hips, cocked an eye toward him and stared. He huffed and then picked up the ark and set it on the floor at the side of the room.

The women brought out plates, cups, and eating utensils, followed by bowls of steaming vegetables and cut fruit. Loaves of bread were set in the middle with urns of water.

Noah motioned for everyone to stand. When the women were finished, they came and stood next to their husbands around the table. Shem squeezed Jazel's hand and then took his mother's hand on the other side of him.

When all held hands, Noah began, "Let us pray."

Shem bowed his head.

His father continued. "Yahweh, maker of all that we see, thank you for providing food for us in abundance. Bless our meal. And thank you for the mercy you are giving to our family. Give us strength to be obedient to this great task. We are your humble servants."

With his eyes closed, and an ear tuned to his father's voice, Shem felt closer to his family than he had in a long time. The questions about how they were going to accomplish this request of Yahweh or if it really was from Yahweh did not seem important. The important thing was that they were all together as a family. It should have brought peace to his heart, but he knew Ham well enough to know division was coming.

Toward the end of the meal, Japheth asked, "Father, how are we to answer when people ask what we are building?"

Noah filled his cup with water and drained it in two gulps.

"We will tell them the truth. Who knows if Yahweh will extend his mercy to any who believe and repent of their vile ways?"

Ham said, "Father, do you not think they will all say we have lost our senses?"

"Probably so," his father mused. "It will not be the first time." He lowered his voice. "But it will definitely be the last."

There was silence as everyone stole glances at each other around the table.

Temani whispered something in Japheth's ear. Japheth looked at Temani and then asked, "Father, the ark is very big. Could we not bring some of our wives' families with us?"

Noah put his cup down and looked around the table at the faces of Jazel, Temani, and Gaddi. Shem felt Jazel tighten her grip on his arm.

"There is room in the ark," he said, "but I am afraid there is no room in their hearts for Yahweh. If they make room for Yahweh, we will make room for them."

"Why does it have to be that way?" Japheth asked.

Noah rose and walked over to a shelf on the wall. He picked up an object from it and returned to the table. He placed it down in front of everyone.

Jazel whispered to Shem. "The bowl with the acorns and the crystal."

Noah smiled at her. "You remember it from my father's dwelling."

"Yes," she said. "It represents the dream your father had."

Noah returned to his stool. "Most of you probably saw this when we went to bury my father. Let me tell you what my father dreamed."

Ham rested his chin on a hand. "Do we have to go over this again?"

His father frowned. "It is important that Gaddi, Temani, and Jazel know what is in the bowl and what it means."

Ham shrugged.

Noah began, "Father dreamed that the first man Yahweh ever created gave him a precious jewel to keep."

Noah picked up the crystal and held it in his hand for all to see.

"But then, drops of water began falling from the sky, and the ground opened up gushing water from below. Soon the water rose all around him covering the ground and plants. As it continued to rise, he feared for the jewel."

Shem watched Jazel. She seemed to hang on every word his father spoke.

"When the water rose higher, my father spotted a wooden bowl with eight seeds in it floating by." Noah picked up the bowl from the table and dropped the crystal in the bowl. "My father placed the jewel in the bowl with the seeds and the bowl floated higher and higher. Soon, the water covered the whole earth and the bowl floated atop it for a long time."

Noah held the bowl up high.

"Eventually, the water receded, and the bowl came to rest on dry ground." He lowered the bowl and placed it on the table again.

"The jewel split into eight pieces and each piece merged with a seed. The seeds were planted in the ground and forests of new trees grew from them, each with a bit of the jewel inside them."

Noah shoved the bowl to the center and dumped the acorns and the crystal out onto the table.

"Do you see the eight acorns? It is easy to conclude that they represent the eight of us at this table."

Jazel squeezed Shem's arm again nodding her head.

He separated the crystal from the acorns. "But what about the jewel? What does it represent?"

Jazel cocked her head still staring at Noah.

"My father," Noah said, "thought he was to go search for the First Man and receive a precious jewel from him."

"The First Man?" Temani asked.

Noah turned toward Temani. "After Yahweh created the world, he created a man and a woman and placed them in a beautiful garden to live. The man, Adam, is known as the First Man. He was still living when my father was a young man."

"When my father finally found him, the First Man shared with him something he had never shared with anyone else.

"It seems the First Man and his wife disobeyed God in that garden causing them, and life as they knew it, to change drastically. That change adversely affected everyone born since."

Gaddi shifted her position, casting glances at the others. "What has changed? I do not see anything wrong with us?"

Shem laughed. "That is because you cannot see as Yahweh sees."

Gaddi shrugged and leaned against Ham.

Jazel rapped Shem's shoulder with her fist.

Noah continued. "Only Yahweh knows how different we are since that first sin. The First Man told my father we were all created to live forever, in Yahweh's presence. But something died inside Adam and his wife when they disobeyed. Now, Yahweh's presence seems non-existent. And like lit candles, our lives eventually flicker and burn out, as my father's has, and as mine, and yours will one day."

Gaddi nestled against Ham. "It does not seem fair that we should be punished for their disobedience."

"We are the product of our parents," Noah said. "See how much you look and act like them. Like it or not, much of them are in you. Why not also this limitation?"

Japheth raised his voice. "But this limitation was not the only thing passed on to us, was it, Father?"

Noah lowered his eyes briefly. "No, Son. Sadly, we also received inside us a nature that actually desires to do what is contrary to Yahweh's wishes.

"I know you all have secretly struggled with these desires. We all have. It has surely not been easy to resist going the way of those living all around us."

Shem fidgeted.

Noah looked at Temani. "That is why we cannot bring anyone, family or friend, who has not made room for Yahweh in their heart. We do not want to plant seeds in the new world that will quickly revert back to their old behavior."

"I do not understand," Jazel said. "How is all *this* represented by a precious jewel? It does not seem precious to me. It is more of a curse."

The smile returned to Noah's face. "You are right, child. What we received as a result of the First Man's disobedience is not precious. But, the First Man told my father, he believes that, because of Yahweh's great love for us, Yahweh is working out a plan to reverse what was done in the garden. Yahweh will make a way to remove our disobedient natures and eliminate death. He will then bring us back into his presence to enjoy everlasting life with him.

"This knowledge, Jazel, is more precious than a jewel. It is this knowledge of Yahweh's love for us that my father wanted us to take and plant into the hearts of our children. They will be the new people of Yahweh. They will live with the knowledge that Yahweh has not abandoned them. They will share the hope of seeing Yahweh defeat death and restore them to his presence."

The table went silent again.

Noah cleared his throat and rose from his stool. "Tomorrow we begin our task. Go home, rest, and remember this time. Your lives will never be the same."

Shem and Jazel made their way toward home. Jazel asked many questions and fantasized aloud about living in the ark and raising children in a new world. Shem pondered the last thing his father said.

How are our lives going to change? What will the people say when they find out what we are doing? Will they treat us differently? How many will want to help and go with us?

Chapter 6

Shem led his team of oxen into the woods. Ham and Japheth, with bare upper bodies, sweated profusely as they labored on opposite sides of a tree, pulling a saw blade back and forth halfway through its trunk.

"Watch your oxen when this one falls," Ham yelled.

"Keep sawing," Shem yelled back. "I will make sure my oxen are not under it when it falls."

Shem pulled on the yoke and moved them out of harm's way toward a felled tree where his father stood atop with an axe.

"One more branch and it's all yours," Noah said as he swung the axe down hard on a protruding limb.

"No need to hurry." Shem leaned against the trunk and inhaled deeply. "Ah, fresh cut wood."

Noah took two more swings and the severed branch fell to the ground. "Now you know how I feel when I am working in my woodshop."

Shem smiled, grabbed a couple ropes, and looked for a place to wrap them around the trunk. He bent down and slid one end of a rope under the tree. Climbing over the trunk, he reached down and pulled the end up and repeated the process with the second rope, wrapping it around the trunk twice. He then secured the other ends to the oxen's harness.

He took the reins and stepped ahead of his oxen. "I have to get this tree out of here before Ham and Japheth drop the next tree. It might block my path."

He moved the team forward until the rope became taut. Then he called to the pair to pull, and the oxen strained briefly, then began pulling the trunk end-wise along the ground. He led them past Ham and Japheth.

"Better hurry!" Ham yelled.

Shem eyed the tree. *Just a little further.* He swatted the rumps of his oxen. "Pull!"

Cra-a-a-ack!

His brothers' tree came crashing down.

Thummmp!

The ground shook next to Shem.

That was close.

***

For almost a moon, Shem's oxen hauled the de-limbed tree trunks out of the woods and onto his father's fields. After so many were scattered across the field, Ham and Japheth stopped felling trees and began cutting the trunks.

They cut them into equal lengths, about two arm-lengths each. These would become the piers for a platform strong enough to hold the entire ark off the ground.

They set the trunk lengths on end and placed them in a row about every five cubits for a span of three hundred cubits. Then they placed another row parallel to the first, and then another row, and another, until they had reached a width of seventy-five cubits.

Once they placed the trunk lengths in rows across the fields, neighbors that had been passing with little notice began to stop at the edge of the fields and talk among themselves.

The men's wives made their way to the field with their daily baskets of assorted fruit, nuts, figs, bread, and water. They placed their bounty on a table edged by two long benches taken from Noah's woodshop.

Shem emerged from the woods leading the oxen with another tree just in time for lunch. He walked over near Japheth, who was on one end of a saw half-way through a tree trunk. Ham handled the saw on the other side.
He stepped into Japheth's line of sight and nodded toward Koz and Arad standing at the other end of the field.

"I do not think they believe we are building a place to put more goats and sheep."

Japheth shook his head. "Why do they not come and ask us what we are doing?"

Ham laughed. "And take a chance to be confronted by Father? I think they will keep their distance.

"Come and eat," their mother called from the table.

Japheth and Ham left their saw halfway through a cut and then joined Shem on his way to the food. Once at the table, they waited for their father, who emerged from between the rows of cut trunks.

"Your father acts like he is out in his woodshop," Henna said. "He is oblivious to everything except what he is working on."

Shem laughed with his brothers. How many times, as children, did they have to go out to his shop and pull Father away from his projects to join them for dinner? He envied his father's passion for his work. At least for this meal, he would forget about the neighbors and enjoy his family.

***

For what seemed like an eternity, Noah and his sons fell more trees, removed the limbs, and hauled them out of the woods.

They took turns on opposite ends of the saws making cuts lengthwise down the tree trunks creating wooden beams. Each beam was then cut to five cubits in length. They laid each beam into a notch they had hewn on the top of each standing platform trunk and extended the other end to a notch in the cut trunk next to it.

Eventually, all the standing trunks were connected by beams both lengthwise and widthwise. This created a waist-high grid supported by the standing trunk sections.

Lastly, they connected the bottom of the standing trunks with planks and diagonals between the trunks to create structural stability to the platform.

Throughout this lengthy process, the villagers had moved a little closer to watch the construction. Shem and his father pulled a saw blade back and forth on a cut down the length of a freshly cut trunk. As Noah pulled the saw his direction, the blade hit a knot-hole and stuck solid. His hands slipped off the handle and he fell backward to the ground.

The villagers laughed.

Shem's anger burned. He grabbed a club-like branch next to the tree and marched up to the crowd. "You laugh now, but who will be laughing later when the water comes and washes you all away."

The crowd became silent.

One of the villagers called out, "What are you talking about? What water?"

Shem had no words to answer them. He felt his face warm. "Go home and mind your own affairs."

Behind him his father's voice rang out. "Son, this *is* their affair."

Shem felt his father's hand on his shoulder. He let the piece of wood drop to the ground.

"People." His father stepped forward and addressed the crowd. "You have watched us for more than a moon cutting these trees and hauling them out to this field. It is time you knew what we are doing."

Shem closed his eyes. *Here it comes.*

"I have spoken to you again and again about returning to the ways of Yahweh, yet you have persisted in doing evil. You refuse to acknowledge the one who created you."

The crowd began to fidget and murmur.

Shem felt the tension rise.

Noah continued, now, projecting his voice louder. "You have exhausted the patience of the Holy One. And Yahweh has decided to wipe you from existence. He is bringing water upon the lands, enough water to flood, not only this whole valley, but all the dry grounds of the earth, higher than the mountains." Noah raised his arms high and turned full circle. "We are building an ark to float atop the coming waters."

The crowd erupted in laughter again.

Someone in the crowd yelled, "Noah, where is all this water going to come from?"

That sounded like Koz. Shem quickly scanned the faces of the crowd.

Noah pointed straight up. "Yahweh will bring it down from the sky and up from under the ground."

The crowd laughed. Some looked up, while most shook their heads.

Another voice sounding like Arad's called out, "I think you hit your head when you fell."

The crowd laughed again.

Noah raised his voice. "You will all perish, but we, who have followed Yahweh will be saved."

The crowd murmured among themselves.

Noah took a step forward. "If you wish to be saved from Yahweh's judgment, repent, and turn from your wickedness. Yahweh may still show you mercy."

Laughter erupted again throughout the crowd.

Shem pulled on his father's arm. "Father, it is too much for them to believe. Come back to work."

The laughing continued as the crowd slowly dispersed. Koz and Arad left last. Noah shook his head and returned to the saw with Shem.

"Father," Shem said, as he reset the saw blade. "We believed your words because of Grandfather's dream. I think they also need more than your words."

Noah hesitated and then took hold of the other end of the saw. "I will try again later."

"Yes, later," Shem said.

Even with the dream, it is hard to believe.

Chapter 7

The oxen snorted as they dragged another tree trunk from the woods. Shem, walked beside one of them, patting it's front shoulder as it strained ahead of the weight. "Almost there, then you both can rest." He counted ten trunks lying on the ground in the cutting area waiting to be cut into planks.

His father approached him. "Ham will be home for a few days forging spikes for the floor of the ark. Take your oxen to their shelter. They have worked enough today."

"You want me to help cut planks from these trunks?"

"No." His father looked eastward and pointed to the mountains. "Prepare a cart, and tomorrow, you and Japheth make your way over those.

"I have heard about a place where steam comes up from below and black tar covers the ground like a lake. Bring back as much as your cart can carry. We have made good progress this season and soon we will need pitch to cover the inside and the outside of the floor."

Shem gazed at the mountains. "I have heard of this place as well...and the stories of strange animals living there."

Noah smiled. "Strong drink and imagination. People love to exaggerate around the fire-pits. I have told Japheth to meet you at your dwelling at sunrise. You should be back by the time Ham is done with his forging."

I wonder how long Ham will drag out his time at the forge.

***

After nearly two days of traveling, Shem and Japheth, leading the mule and cart filled with large tubs, crested the top of the mountain. Shem pulled up on the reigns and gazed across an expanse of mountain tops.

This was his first trek to the top of this one. He could see in every direction. He looked down on the peak above the ridge overlooking his valley. From his dwelling the peak loomed high over the village, an impressive mountain; but from up here it looked so small.

Shem breathed in the cool air. "It is hard to believe that the flood Yahweh is sending will cover all of this, higher than where we are right now."

Japheth stood on the seat taking in the view. He slowly spun until he completely scanned the horizon. "I have never seen so much all at once. Yahweh will need a lot of water to cover that." His voice revealed no trace of doubt.

Shem shrugged and lowered his view to what they were facing. Down the opposite side of the mountain, a thin ridge slowly descended from where they stood, bisecting the area into two separate valleys. Steep cliffs surrounded dense forests in a crater-like valley to the left. Gentle slopes with bare fields, and rocks filled the valley to the right.

Japheth pointed to the valley on the left. "Looks like wisps of smoke or steam rising from the far side of the forest over there."

Shem paused to survey the terrain. "Have you ever been down there before?"

Japheth slowly shook his head. "I have only heard others talk about it."

Shem kept his eyes on the valley. "Do you believe what you heard?"

Japheth raised his shoulders. "Do you?"

Shem patted his brother on the shoulder. "I believe we should camp here for the night and wait until morning to continue."

Japheth surveyed the ground near him. "The grass under that tree looks like a good spot to sleep."

They unhitched the mule from the cart and tied him to a branch near easy nibblings.

By the time the sun set, they had gathered wood, started a fire, and settled in for the night. The forests below slowly disappeared into the shadow of the mountain.

Up early, the brothers guided the mule and cart down the spine of the ridge looking for a way into the forest. The cliffs on the left grew smaller as they descended toward the valley floor. However, after circling half-way around the valley, no trail smooth enough for the cart appeared.

Shem halted the mule opposite a small gap in the cliff walls. He wrapped the mule's tether around a branch. "I think this is as close to the steam as we can get the cart. We are going to have to carry the tubs the rest of the way to the tar."

Japheth looked at the four large tubs on the cart. "Do you think we can carry them full of tar?"

Shem pulled on one of the tubs, threw a small wooden bowl inside it, and hoisted it to his shoulder.

"If we team up and carry only one tub at a time between us, I think we can manage it."

Japheth grabbed another tub and bowl and followed Shem to the gap. They carefully made their way down a rocky ravine with towering sheer rock walls.

As they descended, the walls narrowed to just wider than their shoulders. At the bottom, it opened out into what looked like a flat lakebed surrounded by forest. Steam vapors rose from various depressions in the sandy soil.

Shem felt the air around him warm as they emerged from the opening between the cliff walls. His skin immediately broke into sweat.

Japheth motioned with his chin. "Look, ahead of us."

Shem frowned. "Black sand."

"What do we do?"

Shem felt the heat of the sand increasing through his sandals. "We should approach the tar from those flat rocks on the left."

They moved over to the firmer and slightly cooler ground. The rock slabs led them right to the edge of the tar. They set their tubs near the edge, knelt, and dipped their bowls into the hot tar.

Japheth shook his head. "Whew! These hot fumes smell worse than Father's special mixture of salve oil."

Shem laughed. "It reminds me of Ham's forge."

Japheth lifted his bowl and watched the tar slowly run off into his tub. "I do not think we can ever use these bowls again."

When the tubs were full, the two of them carried one of the tubs to the bottom of the gap in the cliffs.

At the opening, Shem had to turn and back his way up the narrow passage, as Japheth, holding the other side of the tub, followed.

"Next trip," Shem puffed, "you do the backing up."

They repeated the process with two more tubs and lifted them onto the cart. Grabbing the remaining empty tub from the cart, they headed back through the passage.

Back at the tar, filling the tub, Japheth suddenly perked his head up and became ridged.

"What?" Shem said.

Japheth turned his ears to the forest. "Shish! I heard something."

Shem scanned the trees behind them. "Do you have the feeling we are being watched?"

Japheth returned to filling the tub, quickening his pace. "The sooner we get out of here, the better."

With the last tub full, the two hoisted it to their shoulders, one on each side of the tub. As they reached the sandy area, a loud growl, more like a roar, rumbled from within the trees near where they had filled the tubs.

"Keep going!" Shem yelled.

Another growl-roar echoed off the cliff walls ahead of them.

"What is it?" Japheth shouted.

"I do not know. Just keep moving," Shem barked back.

They reached the narrow passage and maneuvered into it as fast as they could, Japheth backing in first, then the tub, then Shem.

Feeling a bit safer in the confines of the passageway, Shem stopped and motioned to set the tub down. He stepped back and poked his head out from the entry of the passageway and looked back toward the tar.

The largest lizard he had ever seen strutted out of the forest. It stood upright on its two hind legs, easily three times their height. It went straight to the two wooden bowls left at the edge of the slab, lowered its gigantic head, and sniffed them.

The lizard raised up, looked straight at Shem, and let loose another roar louder than before.

Shem felt as if his blood turned cold.

He turned toward his brother. "Grab the tub!"

"What is it?" Japheth demanded as he grabbed the handle of the tub.

"Not now. Move! Move!" barked Shem.

They made it through the passage and swung the tub up onto the cart.

Shem snatched the tether, turned the mule and the cart around, and pulled as hard as he could to get the mule moving.

"What was it?" Japheth asked.

"You do not want to know," Shem said.

"But—"

"The next time you hear a story about strange animals at the tar pit—believe it."

Chapter 8

Shem stood on the opposite side of a fallen tree trunk, sharing a saw with his father. They pushed and pulled, cutting down the length of the trunk. Every cubit or so, Shem would stop and insert a flat piece of wood into the gap made by the saw between the trunk and the plank being cut. This kept the weight of the plank from pressing down and jamming the saw.

Shem paused before inserting the next piece of wood into the gap. "I know Japheth is home creating pitch from his beeswax and the tar we brought back, but where is Ham today?

Has he been working his forge all this time? It has been six days since he stayed home to make the floor spikes."

His father hesitated before answering. "I went to see him yesterday to check on his status. We spoke."

Shem shook his head. "You mean, you had words."

"Your brother is strong willed."

"Like his father?"

Noah took a breath as if to answer, but then exhaled instead. "Yes...like his father." He stepped away from the saw and sat on a log behind him.

Shem leaned against the trunk facing his father.

His father looked up with a deep sadness in his eyes. "When am I going to learn?"

Shem had seen those eyes before when Ham and his father butted heads. He brushed the sawdust off his tunic. "I will go talk to him."

His father nodded.

Leaving the saw in the tree and his father sitting on a log, Shem started toward Ham's dwelling.

Once out of sight of his father Shem shook his head. *I cannot believe I am doing this again. When am I going to learn also?*

***

As Shem approached Ham's dwelling, he heard the normal clanging coming from the forge area behind. He circled around back and found Ham, bent over with his back to Shem, hammering on a hot iron rod held with a gloved hand. Shem approached, but before he could call out, Ham spoke between clangs.

"I was waiting for you." He banged the rod one more time before dousing it in a tub of water.

Shem spoke to Ham's back. "Am I that predictable?"

Ham tossed his hammer onto the table next to him and turned around. "You carry the weight of your first-born position on your shoulders."

Anger boiled up within Shem. "I would not have to carry it around so much if you would stop bumping heads with Father."

Ham laughed. "Bumping heads? I was avoiding bumping heads."

Shem raised his voice. "You are neglecting your duty to him."

"My duty?" Ham stood defiantly. "My duty is to provide for my family." He turned, and with his gloved hand, snatched up the rod sticking out of the water tub.

Shem reflexively stepped back.

Ham raised the rod toward Shem. "See this rod. I normally forge two or three tools, a door latch or two, and maybe even a cooking pan each day for people of the village. They give me food and cloth, and sometimes coins in return."

Ham shook the rod. "This rod is the first job I have worked on since Father announced to the people what we were building out there."

Shem walked around Ham and fingered the hammer on the table. "So, you think if you stay away from the construction, your *customers* will return?"

Shem shook his head. "Do you not know that as long as you are part of Father's family, the people will not see you any differently unless you stand in the crowd with them laughing and throwing insults at us as we work? Are you prepared to do that?"

Ham stared back at Shem and then threw the rod back into the water tub. "It is easy to talk now, but wait until your food bin begins to shrink."

"What are you talking about?"

Ham shrugged. "Go home and ask your wife."

Shem threw his hands up in the air. "What is that supposed to mean?"

Ham removed the glove from his hand and walked toward his dwelling. Shem waited for an answer.

"Ham," he shouted after him.

Ham waved him off with a hand. "Go talk to your wife."

"You are as hard-headed as Father." Shem kicked the water tub next to the forge.

Ham entered his home and slammed the door.

"I guess the conversation is over."

What could Jazel possibly know about this? Shem headed home to find the answer.

***

When Shem opened the door, Jazel was coming from the cooking area with the food basket in her hand.

"Oh! I was just bringing you lunch."

Shem hesitated, looking at her smiling face and the sparkle in her eyes. He wished he did not have to be so serious.

"Is something wrong?" she asked.

Not knowing how to begin, he asked, "How are our food bins?"

The smile instantly disappeared from her face. She glanced back into the cooking area and then back at Shem. "What do you mean?"

Shem gently took the basket from her and set it on the table. "I talked with Ham today, and during our conversation he seemed to think that our food supply would soon be dwindling. When I asked him to explain, all he said was to ask you. Is there something you want to tell me?"

Jazel looked down and seemed to deflate. "He has been talking with Gaddi."

"She *is* his wife."

"I did not want you to worry." She looked up at him with eyes that seemed to search his soul. "You have taken on such an overwhelming task that I did not want to weigh you down with more concerns. Gaddi, Temani, and I were going to work it out."

Shem put his hands on her shoulders. "You were going to work what out?"

Jazel stepped back and motioned for Shem to sit. She took a breath and exhaled.

"When you began building, our food bins were full, and the fields were ripe. It was easy to pick what we needed each day and prepare our meals. But we have neglected our fields, and this season they have produced less. So we, Gaddi, Temani, and me, decided to buy the things we needed at the market."

"That sounds reasonable," he said.

"Yes, but since your father pronounced condemnation on the crowd, the people at the market refuse to sell us anything."

"What?" Shem stood. "You should have told me."

"I know, I know." She dropped her head briefly and then looked straight in his eyes. "But we decided we could still get the things we needed another way."

Shem noted that the sparkle was back in her eyes. Intrigued by her resourcefulness, he folded his arms across his chest. "What other way is there?"

Jazel's face betrayed a hint of a smile. "The three of us asked our other families to buy the things we needed. We gave them the coins and they bought food for us."

Shem smiled and shook his head.

"But then," her face changed to serious. "The last time I asked, my father, he refused. He had been drinking and he threatened to retract his agreement for our marriage and bring me back home. He frightened me so much, I have not been back since. Gaddi and Temani shared some of their produce with us."

"Hmmm." Shem ran his fingers through his hair. Now, he understood why Ham was so defensive. "Looks like we need another family meeting."

Jazel grabbed the basket and pulled the cloth off the top. "In the meantime, sit down and eat your lunch."

He patted his wife on the rear and pushed a stool toward her. "You sit and eat also. I am sure all this talk about food has also made you hungry."

She flashed a smile and kicked the stool away. "I do not need a stool when you have a lap."

Suddenly, Shem did not feel like eating.

Chapter 9

When Shem arrived at the construction site the next morning, he could not believe his eyes. There was Ham, helping Japheth unload a tub of pitch from his cart.

As Ham and Japheth carried the tub past him, he heard Ham mutter something about not being ready to stand with the crowd. Shem stared after them and shook his head. *Wonders never cease.*

"Where is Father?" Shem called out.

"I saw him earlier this morning." Japheth puffed under the weight of the tar. "He was headed toward the path to the overlook."

Shem looked up toward the ledge but could not see it well enough from his location. He shrugged.

I hope he is talking to Yahweh.

Japheth and Ham returned to the cart for another container.

"With the three of us," Japheth said. "We should be able to pitch most of the underneath today."

Shem noted two more tubs on the cart. "Is this all the pitch we have?"

Japheth turned a tub handle toward Shem. "No, this is about half of it."

Shem nodded and the two of them slid the tub off the cart and carried it toward the ark.

Shem sniffed the air above the tub. "Your beeswax makes this tar almost bearable. If we need to get more, I think we will ask Ham to forge a couple spears and join us, in case our lizard friend shows up again."

Japheth laughed.

They returned to the cart and Ham stepped forward and helped Shem carry the next one.

As they neared the ark, Shem glanced over his shoulder to make sure Japheth would not overhear. "I talked with Jazel. I understand your concern about the food."

A hint of a smile appeared on Ham's face, but he said nothing.

"Shem! Ham!" Japheth called from the cart. "Father is returning."

They placed their tub next to the other two and returned in time to see Noah waving for them to follow him.

"What now?" Japheth said.

Shem slapped him on the back as he passed. "I hope it has to do with food."

The three brothers followed their father to his garden behind his dwelling. The soil, almost bare of vegetables, was overrun with weeds. Only a few squash plants had anything still growing on them.

"Father," said Shem. "Your garden looks like mine."

"Yes, no doubt we have all neglected our personal needs to work on the ark. I have sought Yahweh on this, and he has spoken."

Shem caught Ham's eye before looking to his father.

"Yahweh says, this season plant all our fields. Until now you have only planted in certain areas. Till the soil and plant vegetables and grain in every available space you can find, even up to the boundaries of your property."

"Father," Shem spoke up. "We need food now. Our food bins are low. We have neglected our gardens the same as you while building. The people in the market will not sell to us. How are we going to make it until harvest?'

Noah frowned, and then, as if a lamp shone from behind his eyes, he spoke. "Yahweh says that because you have neglected your own fields to work on his ark, he will provide for your personal needs himself. Your food bins will not run out as you build. You will not have to buy, beg, or borrow as you set your attention to his will.

"Of every six days, you will set aside two to work your fields and gardens. The seventh day shall remain a day of rest. Yahweh will sustain you as you look to him."

Shem and his brothers exchanged glances.

"Father," Japheth said. "So, all we have to do is to trust Yahweh?"

Noah nodded. "Yes."

Ham lowered his head and slowly shook it.

Shem stepped forward. "What happens if we do as Yahweh asks and we run out of food?"

Ham jerked his head up.

Noah did not flinch. "It will not happen. But I see you may need some encouragement in your faith." Noah paused and looked all three of them in the eyes. "Test Yahweh on this. Do as he says and be in awe. Then you will know for sure that what Yahweh says, he will do. We will all need our faith to be strong for what is to come."

Shem did not know what to think. *Will Yahweh really put food in our bins? How can such a thing happen?*

"Father," Japheth asked. "Why do we need to plant so much? Our properties are larger than we need. We will have too much for our families."

His father smiled. "Because, at the rate we are building, by next harvest the ark will be ready to inhabit. The animals boarding with us will also need to eat. You will be growing food for them as well as for us."

"Animals?" Shem asked.

"Did you forget why the ark is so big?"

Shem felt his face warm.

His father placed his hand on Shem's shoulder as he stepped past him.

"We will have at least two of every animal on the earth with us." He continued toward the ark leaving Shem and his brothers standing silent. Before he got out of earshot, he called over his shoulder. "When your faith is stronger, you will believe."

Japheth moved first. "Come. Let us pitch the ark and worry about the animals later."

Shem knew he was right. "Come on Ham. We can pitch and then go home and look at our bins."

Ham followed behind shaking his head.

***

At lunch time, the women arrived and set out the mid-day meal. The men gathered at the table, thanked Yahweh for the food, and started eating.

Their mother laughed. "I do not know which has more pitch on it, the ark or you men."

Japheth held up one of his tarred arms. "Will this make it easier for me to float?"

Temani giggled. "If you come home like that it will be easier for you to sleep outside."

Shem noted that the mood at the table seemed light and more comfortable than usual. He wondered if it was due to the talk earlier. Eventually the women began cleaning up, and the men started back to work.

Shem leaned close to Jazel, careful not to touch her with his tarred hands.

"Did you notice anything unusual with the food bins when you prepared our meal?"

Jazel cocked her head. "Unusual? No, nothing. The food bins are the same as always—almost empty. Why?"

"I thought…oh, no reason." Shem headed toward the ark. "I will see you when I get home tonight."

I want to believe Father, but sometimes he says things… Shem shook his head and refocused on the tar waiting for him under the ark.

Another day of bending over under the ark. My back is going to be sore tonight.

***

Later that night, Shem spent a longer-than-normal time washing the tar off his face and arms before coming to the table for dinner.

"It is about time," Jazel said as she placed a steaming bowl in front of him. "I had to warm your lentils over the fire a second time."

Shem sat and held his bare arms out. "It took a while to get the tar off."

Jazel inspected them. "I guess they are clean enough to eat with."

He closed his arms around her waist and caressed her. "Are they clean enough to hold you?"

"Yes." She squirmed free.

"But I do not want to reheat your lentils a third time. They will be soft like mush. Put those clean hands around your bowl. And, by the way, thank you for finding us some more potatoes and beets. I will fix them for you tomorrow."

Shem choked on the lentils. "I did not dig any potatoes or beets from the garden. Are you sure there are more than before?"

"Of course, I am sure." She laughed. "I know my own food bins."

Shem rose from the stool. "Show me the potatoes."

"Do not be so silly. They are just potatoes."

He marched into the cooking room and opened the lid to one of the food bins. "Which bin?"

"The bin on the end." Jazel waged her head. "What is the matter with you?"

He lifted the lid and pulled out a couple potatoes. "Hmmm. These are not from our garden."

"How can you tell?"

"These potatoes are bigger and much heartier than the ones we grow." Shem held the potatoes out to show Jazel. "No one came by to see you today?"

"No, I was by myself all day. Shem, you are scaring me. What is this all about?"

He took her by the hand, led her to the eating table, and motioned for her to sit. He pulled a stool close and sat next to her. He explained the meeting they had with his father earlier that morning. He told her about how his father said Yahweh would provide for them as they built the ark.

"I was not going to tell you because I did not know what to believe. You know how Father is."

She took one of the potatoes from Shem and inspected it. "Do you really think Yahweh put these potatoes in our food bin?"

He inhaled. "Well, I did not put them there, and you did not put them there, so it must have been Yahweh."

Jazel's face lit up. "Thank you, Yahweh."

Shem could not sit anymore. He got up and paced the room.

"Do you know what this means Jazel?"

He did not wait for her to answer. "It means Yahweh really spoke to Father. Yahweh is really going to bring flood waters to destroy the people. It also means…Yahweh has chosen to save us…you, me, and my family, from the destruction to come."

Shem knelt in front of Jazel and took her hands. "Yahweh really cares for us. Yahweh, who created the earth and everything we see, cares for us, *personally*." He looked into Jazel's eyes and tears welled up blurring his vision of her. "I feel ashamed for doubting."

He wiped his eyes with his sleeve and saw that Jazel's face was just as tearful as his. He laid his head on her lap and hugged her waist. She stroked his hair as she cried.

It was only a few potatoes and beets, but they revealed something greater than Shem could have imagined. Their creator cared for them.

Chapter 10

The next few weeks, the work felt lighter and the days moved by faster. Shem heard more laughter from his brothers. Ham even seemed jovial at times.

At first Shem did not share about the extra food in his bin. What if the others did not receive anything? He would appear to be boasting.

Eventually, their father asked them as they were erecting an inside wall section. "I have not heard any complaints about a lack of food since our last talk. Did Yahweh provide as I said he would?"

Shem and his brothers traded glances and then all burst out laughing and told how various vegetables and fruit would appear in their food bins overnight.

Sometimes there would be squash, or tubers, or carrots in a bin that had nothing the day before.

Sometimes mushrooms, figs, or dates would be in another bin. The flour levels never seemed to go down, and the flasks of olive oil were full each morning.

Their father walked away laughing.

Shem and his brothers worked two days on the ark and then one in their fields or gardens and then two on the ark and one at home again. In this way, all the fields were planted, the animals cared for, and the work on the ark continued through the growing season.

As the walls were erected, the ark slowly dominated the landscape. Not even in the village stood a structure so massive--three hundred cubits of tarred walls as high as the trees. They built rooms three times as deep as an entire dwelling, all mounted atop a waist-high platform lying in an open crop field, a moon's walk away from any body of water large enough to float it.

For a long time, Shem ignored the villagers that stared from a distance. But now, when he looked at the crowd, he saw mostly unfamiliar faces. *Word must be spreading. People must be coming from neighboring villages to see what we are building.*

***

Shem and Ham and Japheth each carried a ladder to the ark. They entered the single opening of the ark about three times wider than a normal dwelling's doorway, and twice as high, cut into the wall of the ark.

The door, hinged at the bottom, lay open as a ramp down to the ground. Once inside, they ascended a ramp straight to a second floor about ten cubits above. This floor extended the length of the ark and to both sides. Stalls of various sizes lined the walls all around this second level with enclosed rooms for food storage every ten stalls.

Japheth and Shem walked to the center of the floor and looked down an opening edged by a railing. It measured about five cubits wide extending two hundred cubits down the length of the ark.

Japheth looked above them at a similar opening in the middle of the floor above. "Those openings sure give an open feeling in here. The birds are going to enjoy it."

"Yes," Ham said, as he placed the ladder he carried against the railing, connecting the upper deck to the middle deck. "It also allows easy deck to deck communication." He began securing the bottom of the ladder to the railing.

Shem laughed. "And it makes it harder for you to hide."

Ham shrugged and hammered the top of the ladder to the floor of the deck above him.

"I may not be able to hide," he said. "But I can slip up or down a ladder in the blink of an eye and make you look for me."

In two quick steps, Ham disappeared onto the deck above.

Shem waited, and when Ham did not reappear, he shook his head. "Come on Japheth. Our ladders go at the other end. Ham will turn up later."

Japheth smiled. "You walked right into that one."

After installing their ladders, Shem and Japheth took the ramp up to the third floor another ten cubits higher. Laughter came from the area forward of the ramp. They entered the eating room and found their wives with Gaddi and a smug looking Ham.

Jazel, with a twinkle in her eyes, pulled on Shem's sleeve. "We have seen the food preparation area. We were waiting for our husbands to see our sleeping rooms."

Temani and Gaddi both laughed. The three couples disappeared into separate rooms briefly and then gathered again in the common eating area.

Gaddi quipped loud enough for the men to hear, "These men think these rooms are big enough to put all our personal things in."

Temani chimed in. "Did they forget how much we all have?"

Jazel smirked. "Men. What goes on in their heads?"

Everyone laughed.

Noah entered and called them into the food preparation room. He pointed to a low spot on the floor.

"Ham, what is the status on the fire-plate?"

"I have it done and will drop it in tomorrow."

"Good." Noah patted Ham on the shoulder, took a step back, and looked at his three sons. "We have not lived this close since you were small boys."

"Yes," Shem pushed Japheth. "And we fought almost every day."

His father shook his head. "Any fighting will be done on the other end of the ark."

They all walked over to the railing and gazed down through large opening at the decks below. Noah put his hands on his hips. "Yahweh be praised. Looks like we are about done."

***

Shem dropped an armful of rocks from the stream into a recessed area in the cooking room where Ham, down on his hands and knees, was working.

"Is that enough?"

Without looking up, Ham slid the rocks up against other rocks he had brought in.   "Yes, this will create a buffer between the wood floor and the fire-plate I made."

He pointed to a shallow iron bowl about two cubits in diameter he had forged and hammered. "We do not want the women to burn a hole in our floor while cooking our meals."

Shem brushed the dust off his hands. "Ah, the advantage of having a brother with a forge."

Japheth came up the ramp and entered the room just in time to help Ham and Shem lift the iron fire-plate down onto the rocks.

"Hold it steady," Ham said as he let go of the bowl. "I need to adjust a couple rocks."

"Hurry," Japheth said. "This is heavy."

Shem grimaced. "It is not that heavy."

"I think my side," Japheth puffed, "is heavier than your side."

Ham shook his head. "You whiners can set it down now."

Both brothers set the fire-plate down and immediately put their hands on their hips and arched their backs.

"I just came from outside," Japheth said. "There seem to be more strangers in the crowd now that the walls are up."

"Yes," Shem said. "I think they are coming from the neighboring villages."

"Yesterday," Ham said. "One of them asked me if we were building a temple to a new god."

Shem put his hands half-way up. "Do not tell Father. He will start preaching to them again."

Japheth frowned at Shem.

"I am just kidding."

"Oh, I meant to tell you." Japheth put his hand on Shem's shoulder. "A little while ago I saw Jazel's father in the crowd. He was standing next to one of the Bardo brothers, Koz, I think."

Shem frowned. "Why would he be here?"

"Maybe he wants to talk to you."

Shem headed toward the ramp. "I will go see what he wants."

Shem walked down the ramp to the next floor and then down the next ramp and stopped at the door. Scanning the crowd, he could not see Jazel's father or Koz among any of the people watching.

Oh well. If he wants to talk, he knows where I am.

***

Shem leaned against a fence post and surveyed his sheep and goats. They looked stout and healthy, probably better than they had ever looked. He turned and viewed the vegetable garden, bursting with produce. His brother's grain fields were ready to harvest, and Japheth's trees bent under the weight of ripening fruit.

Harvest time and the ark was finally finished, just as his father had said. Yahweh had blessed their work as he had promised.

Shem and his family began cutting the stalks of grain and threshing them right there in the field. They collected the seeds into baskets and stored them away on the upper deck of the ark. The stocks were then gathered and spread on the floors of the stalls on the second deck.

They used ladders to pick fruit from Japheth's trees and loaded it along with produce from the gardens onto a cart and had the mule haul it to the ark. They then cut large branches off some of the trees and carried them up to the stalls on the third deck for the birds to roost in.

Shem helped Ham store his forge and tools aboard, but watched from a safe distance as Japheth carefully moved his beehives onto the ark.

He marveled that during all this work not a single person from the village watched. Harvest time demanded everyone's focus to be on their own fields. It seemed ironic to Shem that the villagers labored in their fields to secure a future that would never come.

***

Next morning Jazel called from the back window of their home. "Shem, your father has called a meeting."

Shem patted the back of the goat feeding next to him and started toward the dwelling. "I am on my way."

He met Jazel at the front door and they walked together to his father's home. Japheth, Ham, and their wives arrived just ahead of them. Henna motioned for all to sit at the eating table where she had placed a plate of sliced bread, cups, and a jug of juice.

Noah entered the room and stood at the end of the table. His eyes seemed excited, but he spoke with a controlled tone. "Yahweh has spoken to me. The time has come."

Chapter 11

Shem took a breath and squeezed Jazel's hand.

Noah spread his arms wide. "We are to take from our homes everything we need and load it onto the ark. Starting this day, the ark will be our home."

Shem traded glances with Japheth and Ham.

"Yahweh has commanded all the animals in the land to come to us to be saved. We will put two of every animal, a male and its mate, on board and seven pairs of male and female animals that are good for sacrifices. Shem, bring your goats and your sheep and secure them in the stalls and pens we made."

"And my oxen?" Shem asked.

"Yes, your oxen too."

Shem nodded.

"Yahweh has also commanded every kind of bird to come to us. We are to put seven pairs of each kind aboard to keep them alive as well. We will put them in the stalls with the tree branches on the upper deck.

"In seven days, Yahweh will open the floodgates of heaven, and for forty days and forty nights he will rain down water upon the earth. The floodwaters will rise higher than the highest mountain and will wipe from the face of the earth every living creature he has made."

"Ohhh!" Temani buried her head in Japheth's tunic and began sobbing.

Noah nodded to Henna.

"There, there," Henna bent down and put her hand on Temani's shoulder. "What is it child?"

Temani lifted her head. "What about my family? My sister, Galal, and her little girl?"

Henna looked up at Noah with pleading in her eyes.

"Child," Noah said. "We have room on the ark if you can convince them to come."

"I have tried." She buried her head again and sobbed.

Shem looked at Jazel.

Jazel lowered her head. "I have asked my family as well, but they laugh at me. They will not come."

"Neither will mine," Gaddi said.

Shem spoke more to everyone than to just Jazel. "Maybe when they see all the animals coming to us they will change their minds."

Noah slowly shook his head. "Maybe."

***

That afternoon, as Jazel packed her food preparation utensils, Shem loaded the cart with stools, tables, and other heavier items. They moved everything to the ark and placed most of their things into their personal room. The tables and stools were placed in a common area near the food preparation area.

They made one last trip to their dwelling to decide what else to take and what to leave behind.

"Do you want this old water tub?" Shem called from just outside the back doorway.

"Leave it behind," Jazel shouted back. "You will make me a new one when we get to our new home."

Shem looked the tub over, shook his head, and then tossed it on a pile of leave-behind items next to the wall. After inspecting the goat pens, he re-entered the dwelling and found Jazel standing in the opening between the, now-vacant, eating area and the food preparation room. She stood motionless, staring at the fire pit.

He softly put his hand on her back. "Is everything alright?"

She turned and leaned into him, a tear escaping down her cheek. "I cannot believe we are really leaving."

He hugged her. "I know. We were very happy here. And we will be very happy in our new home. Come. Let us get back to the ark. It is getting late."

That night, the four couples assembled in the eating area for their first meal aboard the ark.

When everyone was seated, Noah stood and raised a hand. The others gave him their attention.

"This is the first of many meals we will share in the ark. Let us give thanks."

Shem took Jazel's hand and bowed his head.

"Yahweh, we are thankful for your mercy in the midst of judgement. We eat this meal with excitement thinking about the future. But also, with sadness thinking about the people around us. We are in your hands. Oh…Yes…I also pray that you will make good any mistakes we made building your ark."

Everyone laughed and began eating.

After the meal and the initial excitement of being together subsided, Shem and Jazel eventually retired to their new room to sleep.

Jazel fidgeted in bed. "This is much smaller than our room at home."

Without raising his head from the pillow. "It is just temporary."

"We have no window to let fresh air in."

"With the air would come water. It is better this way. Go to sleep"

"I do not think I can sleep."

Shem raised his head and sighed. "Do you want to talk?"

Jazel sat up and swung her feet onto the floor. "I have been thinking about what your father prayed before the meal...about being sad for the people around us."

"What about it?" He propped himself up with his elbow.

"When the ark was finished, I was excited. But when we moved all our belongings out of our dwelling and into the ark, I was saddened to be leaving. But now, I realize that we are not the ones leaving. The people around us are leaving. We are just staying inside the ark until Yahweh washes the people away, like cleaning food scraps off a plate. Now I am sad...no...angry that my family has become...food scraps." She got up and began pacing next to their bed. "What if Yahweh becomes angry with us after we start over? Will we become scraps to be washed away too?"

Shem sat on the edge of the bed. "You are forgetting about the jewel in the bowl." He patted the bed next to him for her to sit. "Come here."

She sighed and sat. "What does the jewel have to do with this?"

"Remember, the jewel broke into pieces and joined with the eight seeds and produced new forests after the flood. We are part of Yahweh's plans. He loves us. He will not use us and then toss us aside. That is why the jewel is so precious. It represents Yahweh's love, which, according to the First Man, endures forever.

"Your family has rejected Yahweh and his love. That should make you sad, and angry at them, not Yahweh."

Tears streaked down Jazel's cheeks.

Shem rubbed her back. "Grieving for your family shows you love them. Father never said Yahweh was angry with the people, only sad. I think Yahweh also grieves that only eight of us are in the ark."

Jazel dried her cheek on Shem's shoulder. "I am ready to go to sleep now."

***

Shem rose early and went down the ramps and met Japheth standing in the middle of the ark's opening.

Japheth pointed to the fields.

Shem looked outside and had to grab ahold of Japheth's arm to keep from stumbling backward. The field in front of them was filled with all sorts of animals. Most were sitting motionless on the ground, some on logs, and some paced as if they were waiting for something.

The trees at the edge of the woods were bursting with birds of all sizes and colors. Shem recognized some of them, but most he had never seen before.

"Where did they come from?" Japheth whispered.

Shem smiled. "Not from anywhere close by. Father said that Yahweh commanded the animals from all over the land to come to us."

"Yes," Japheth said. "But I had no idea there would be…this many…and so many different kinds."

Shem scanned the field. "I do not see our lizard friend anywhere."

Japheth turned around and ran up the ramp. "I am going to get the others."

Minutes later, Japheth returned followed by the rest of the family. They all stopped at the opening and stared out at the fields.

Temani held to her husband. "They scare me."

Jazel tip-toed down the ramp and slowly edged toward them. "They are beautiful, all different sizes and colors.

"Be careful," Gaddi called to her.

Shem looked at his father and whispered. "Are they safe?"

Noah laughed. "They are our new neighbors, provided by Yahweh. Of course, they are safe."

A spot-covered cat larger than one of their goats rose from sitting and slowly approached Jazel. She drew her hands up high and froze as the cat came up to her.
The cat sniffed her feet and then rubbed its head against her legs. She slowly lowered her hands and stroked the animal's fur.

"She is so soft."

The others descended the ramp and started walking slowly amongst the animals. Most of the animals ignored them. Some of them sniffed, or snorted, but none seemed agitated or afraid.

Shem approached a pair of tall, long-necked, orange and brown spotted animals. His head only came to the top of their legs, with their necks stretching the same amount of distance higher. "We will have to put these two in the middle under the opening between the decks."

"Well, sons," Noah said. "What are you waiting for? Start leading them to their stalls."

Ham surveyed the birds in the trees. "This could take days."

His father looked up at the sky. "Yahweh has given us six."

***

Shem found that with very little nudging the animals responded and allowed themselves to be led up the ramp and into the ark. The heavier ones were put on the lower deck and the lighter ones were led up the other ramps to the higher decks.

Japheth yelled out. "I hope we built the floor strong enough for these two." He walked ahead of two giant hairless creatures, each the size of two of Shem's oxen. With legs like tree stumps and ears like giant leaves, the two animals followed him closely. The one directly behind him continuously reached out with his long snout and pushed it against the back of Japheth's shoulder.

"I think he wants you to walk faster," Shem shouted.

Ham moved a pair of furry little creatures that each held one of his hands. They walked somewhat upright on short, bowed, hairy legs. As he passed Shem, he whispered. "Have you noticed the people of the village?"

Shem looked past Ham to the edge of the field. "Yes. They do not come as close as they usually do."

Ham said, "And they hide behind trees and bushes, watching only briefly before leaving. They act as if they are afraid."

Shem laughed. "I was afraid when I first saw the field from the ark this morning."

Ham stared at the field's edge. "I think trouble is coming."

"You worry too much." Shem turned and headed toward a pair of small long-snouted animals with sharp pin-like hair instead of fur. He decided to use a stick to maneuver them toward the ark.

As he approached the opening, Japheth came down the ramp. He had a smile from ear to ear.

"What is with you?" Shem asked.

Without slowing, Japheth shook his head. "I do not know when I have had so much fun. These animals are so unique, they make me laugh."

Shem yelled back after he passed. "You think they are funny? Try leading that pair of giant green lizards over near the trees. They are all mouth and tail."

Japheth waved an acknowledgement.

Two days later, Japheth rushed up to Shem as he led a pair of small, black and white striped horses toward the ramp. He had no smile on his face.

He spoke before Shem could ask him anything. "I just saw Bardo and his sons at the edge of the field."

Shem strained his eyes in that direction. "Go get Father."

A robust man, clad in bright yellow robes, flanked by Arad and Koz, strode across the field toward the ark. The glare of the sun reflecting off Bardo's necklaces, wrist guards, and other metal trimmings gave him the appearance of a fireball marching toward them.

A crowd of villagers followed close behind. Bardo's sons shoved or kicked any smaller animals to the side that blocked their way.

Shem steadied the pair of striped horses and kept them to the side of the ramp between him and the commotion.

Bardo slowed his steps and stopped short of the ramp. The small crowd stopped a short distance behind him surveying the ark. The big man glared over at Shem, huffing and puffing, with reddened face and eyes that seemed ready to explode.

Chills ran down Shem's spine.

His father appeared in the ark's opening with Japheth and Ham. Bardo looked up at Noah, opened his mouth, and shouted, "Noah, this must come to an end."

Shem mused. *If you only knew...*

Chapter 12

Bardo was a huge man, a head taller than everyone else. The perfect centerpiece of the crowd. Shaking his head as he examined the ark, he lifted the edges of his bright yellow cloak and let them drop to lay flat against his curved torso.

Shem steadied the two animals in front of him and glanced at Bardo's two sons. *Arad and Koz are looking more smug than usual.*

"Noah." The big man cleared his throat, then spoke a little softer than before. "The villagers have been very patient and tolerant with you and your family these past few seasons. They stood by and suffered much embarrassment as people from other villages made fun of them because of this...this..."

"Ark," Noah said.

The edge of Bardo's lips hinted at a smile. "Yes…this ark." Then his brows furled and red reappeared on his cheeks. He raised his voice. "But now you have gone too far with these…animals. They scare my people and eat their crops. I do not know how you got them to come to you, and I do not care, but you must send them away."

Noah's face shifted from sternness to sadness.

"Bardo." Noah spoke loud enough for the crowd to hear. "If you knew what was coming, you would follow these animals into the ark. Yahweh is bringing—"

"We do not want to hear about what your Yahweh is bringing," Bardo barked back. "If all these animals are not gone from here in three days…" Bardo motioned toward the crowd with his arms. "These people and I will be bringing torches. Your ark has so much pitch, no amount of water Yahweh could bring will be able to extinguish the fire we will start."

Bardo and Noah stared silently at one another, and then Bardo turned and marched through the crowd back the way he came. The crowd murmured and then followed, leaving Arad and Koz standing at the bottom of the ramp.

Koz looked straight at Shem. "You heard what my father said--three days."

Arad laughed. "Or…there will be enough roasted meat to feed the whole village."

The two casually walked away, sneering at the animals they passed. Soon they disappeared into the woods.

Shem looked up at his father.

Noah shook his head. "These people do not know what they are doing."

Shem found himself shaking his head also. He patted the striped rump of one of the horses and led them up the ramp past Japheth and Ham.

"Father," Japheth said. "Are not the waters to come on the third day from today?"

"Yes." He turned back into the ark. "Bardo's wishes will be honored. The animals will surely be gone from here in three days."

***

Early on the third morning, Shem pulled the covers over his head trying to block a way-too-early noise from across the room.

"Shem," Jazel called out.

He squeezed the covers tighter.

"Shem, I know you are awake."

Shem knew she would not stop until he answered. "Mmmm," he mumbled as he pulled the covers from his face and slightly opened his eyes.

Jazel was rummaging through some sacks on the floor near the wall in their new quarters.

"Shem, have you seen the wreath you made for me for our wedding? It was hanging on the outside of the back door."

"Ah...I did not touch it. You must have misplaced it."

"No," she said. "I have not seen it since we moved. It must still be hanging on the door."

He pulled the covers back over his face. "Maybe so."

Shem heard the door open.

"I am going back to our dwelling and get it. I will be right back."

"Mmmm."

The door closed.

Later, Shem got up and went into the eating room. Henna, Gaddi and Temani were preparing food near the fire pit. His father and Ham sat at the table.

His father looked at him. "Hard to get up this morning?"

Shem nodded.

Ham held his spoon and pointed at him. "You should not have stayed up so late watching those animals."

Shem took the stool next to Ham and sat. "There are so many different kinds. I never tire looking at them."

Temani placed a bowl of hot lentils and rice in front of Shem.

Shem looked up at her. "Thank you."

Japheth, branding a big smile, entered the room from the opening facing the ramp. "The fields are empty this morning."

"All the animals must be in the ark," their father said. "Everyone stay close to the ark today. I do not know how or when Yahweh will bring the water."

Shem looked into the food preparation room. "Where is Jazel?"

"I saw her outside earlier this morning," Japheth said. "She was walking toward the edge of the field."

"Where would she be going?" Noah asked.

Shem stared down at his bowl trying to remember what she had said. "She mentioned something about the wreath I made her. I think we left it at home."

"If she went to look for it," Japheth said. "She should have been back by now."

Shem shoveled a couple spoonsful of lentils into his mouth and shoved the bowl aside. "I will go see what is taking her so long."

He descended the ramps and started across the field. The multitude of birds that had been perched in the trees the last few days were taking flight. Shem watched as they circled above him. Groups of birds began breaking away from the larger group, swooping down near the ground, and flying into the opening of the ark.

I was wondering how we were going to get all those birds into the ark.

Focusing back on his task, Shem headed toward his dwelling. As he approached the open front door, there in the dirt before the porch lay the wreath Jazel had come to get. He stooped and picked it up. It looked disheveled, like it had been stepped on.

Shem's stomach tightened. "Jazel!"

He ran inside. "Jazel!"

He hurried from room to room and then looked out the back door. "Jazel! Are you here?"

The silence brought chills up his spine. *I need help.*

He ran back to the ark, ducking birds as he ascended the ramps. Out of breath, he burst into the eating area. Everyone was still in the room.

"What is it?" his father asked.

"Jazel is gone. I found the wreath..." He held the wreath out and caught his breath. "But no Jazel. Someone has taken her."

Gaddi stepped closer and fingered the wreath softly. "Back when you were building the ark, Jazel mentioned that her father threatened to take her back home because of the shame we were bringing her family."

Japheth slammed the table with his fist. "I saw Jazel's father in the crowd speaking with Koz a while back. I bet he arranged this with the Bardo brothers."

"The Bardo brothers?" Shem started for the door. "We need to get her back."

"Wait!" His father grabbed Shem's arm and gently removed the wreath from his hand. "Where are you going, to Jazel's father's home or to Bardo's?"

Shem's mind swirled as he brushed his hair back with both hands. He had not gotten that far in his thoughts.

Ham spoke up. "I think they will be at Jazel's father's home."

"Good," Noah said. "I must stay here in case Bardo and the crowd returns. Remember, you must be back before the rain begins. May Yahweh give you speed."

***

The three brothers ran down the ramp and crossed the now vacant field. Shem noticed the sky had darkened considerably, and the air felt thick to him. He had no time to think about that now. They cut through the woods toward Jazel's parents' dwelling. Images of Jazel drowning in the flood waters flashed through Shem's mind. He knew her father would not intentionally hurt her, but unless he could rescue her, she would be lost along with all the others.

They cleared the woods, crossed a recently harvested field, and stopped, out of breath, in front of a home. Memories of his and Jazel's wedding ceremony came flooding into his mind.

Ham looked at Shem with darkened eyes. "Do you want me to break down the door?"

Shem held his hand up. "Jodak!" he shouted. "Open the door."

They heard a rustling from inside, and then the door opened. Jodak, a short stocky man, stepped out onto the porch followed by a much larger Koz and Arad. They crossed their arms and stared at Shem.

Shem cast a glance at the two Bardo brothers and then addressed Jodak. "We do not want anyone to get hurt. We just want Jazel."

Jodak, with brows furled, moved forward to the edge of the porch. "I gave you my daughter in good will, thinking that you would care for her. Instead, you have shamed her." He pointed his stubby finger at Shem. "You have brought shame on my family as well." He slapped his chest hard with an open hand. "I have taken her back so she and my family will be respected again."

Shem clenched his jaw. "We will take her by force."

Koz stepped to the edge next to Jodak and smiled. "It has been a long time since Arad and I have thrashed the sons of Noah."

Japheth and Ham edged forward.

Arad moved next to his brother. "It will be like old times. Helim! Irodi!"

More sounds came from inside. The door opened and two more men stepped from the dwelling.

Shem's heart sank.

Just then a drop of water landed on Shem's cheek. He looked up. Another drop hit his forehead. Chills ran up his spine. He looked at Japheth and Ham. They held their hands out catching drops of water as well.

The drops came faster.

"We need her now!" Shem demanded.

"What is this?" Koz yelled as he held out a hand spotted with water droplets.

"This is the beginning of the end for you," growled Ham as he stepped toward Koz.

The ground rumbled and the dwelling shook.

The men on the porch seized the railing to steady themselves. Something inside crashed and the door of the dwelling burst open. Jazel exploded past the men, hurling herself headlong off the porch, crumpling into the dirt.

The ground shook again. Shem and his brothers collapsed to the ground. As the ground continued to move, Shem pulled himself on his stomach toward Jazel. A large crack broke the ground near her feet.

"Aiiaaa!" Jazel screamed.

The crack widened into a crevice. The shaking increased and Jazel began sliding, feet first, toward the edge.

"Shem!" she cried.

Shem extended his arms toward her. "Grab my hand!"

She stretched an arm in Shem's direction. He managed to snatch it on the first try. He squeezed it hard, straining with all he had in him, and pulled her toward him. When he had slid her a little closer, he took her other hand, heaved hard, and drew her next to him. Water began pouring from the crack and covering the ground.

The shaking subsided, but the rain increased in strength.

Shem jumped up and helped Jazel to her feet. The men on the porch still clung to the railing looking up at the sky.

"Ham! Japheth!" Shem shouted above the sound of the rain. "Back to the ark!"

The fissure between Shem and the porch widened and the water quickly engulfed the dwelling. Shem, Jazel, and his brothers ran for the open field, rain pelting their faces. Once in the woods, the trees blocked most of the rain. Shem and the others slowed their pace.

Shem noticed red on the front of Jazel's rain-soaked tunic. "Are you hurt?"

"Just a few scrapes. I will be fine once we get back on the ark."

The ground rumbled again, but not as much as before.

Japheth looked up at the darkened sky above the trees. "I think we need to hurry."

They ran until they reached the edge of the field facing the ark.

"We are almost there," Shem shouted.

Ham pulled on Shem's arm. "Wait. Look over there."

A crowd carrying torches lined the edge of the woods. Still the rain fell.

Shem scanned the crowd. "I think they are waiting for Bardo. Come on. We need to beat them to the ark."

They began running toward the ark. Bardo's bright yellow tunic appeared in front of the crowd yelling something that Shem could not understand through the sounds of the rain. The crowd surged forward into the field. More torches appeared.

Noah stood at the top of the ramp waving wildly.

The ground rumbled again beneath the soaked field. Large cracks appeared spewing water into their path. Shem and the others had to high step through shin high water.

Some of the crowd fell back and fled into the woods. Bardo, with torch held high, still yelling orders, continued with a few determined souls slogging through the watery mess.

Shem and the others reached the ramp and quickly ascended into the ark. Temani and Gaddi sobbed as they received Japheth and Ham into their arms. Henna, with tears running down her cheeks, put her arms around both Jazel and Shem and held them tightly. Shem felt like a baby chick under the protective wings of its mother.

Immediately, the ramp, which was hinged to the bottom of the opening, began to rise. They all stared in awe. It rose as if a giant invisible hand was lifting it.

Yahweh?

Chapter 13

As the ramp rose, through the narrowing gap, Shem watched Bardo, alone now, and up to his waist in water. He hurled his torch at the opening. It fell a few cubits short and floated, flames extinguished, on the surface of the water. The last Shem saw before the door closed completely was Bardo, bent down by the force of the rain, retreating toward the woods.

The eight of them stood in silence staring at the former ramp, now upright and firmly secured into the frame of the opening.

"We are safe now," Noah said. "Gaddi and Temani, take the oil flasks from the supply room and make sure the lamps on all decks are full. This is going to be a long night."

Henna tugged lightly on Jazel's tunic. "Change into dry clothes and I will look at your leg."

Noah pointed to the ceiling. "Japheth, there is a pot of pitch hanging above the fire in the cooking room. Remove the pot and bring it down here to pitch around this door. Shem, take some of the pitch and inspect the lower deck for water leaks. Ham, you do the same for the upper deck ceiling. I will be attending our *guests*."

Shem followed Japheth and Ham up to the fire-pit. No one spoke about how the door of the ark closed. The pitch bubbled in the pot above the fire. After scooping a portion into two smaller containers, Shem picked up one, grabbed an oil lamp, and went down to the lower deck to begin searching for water leaks.

It felt eerie in the dark down on the bottom deck. Shem heard a low sounding tone echoing off the walls mixing with the sound of the rain beating against the outside. He moved past several animal pens. The tones became clearer, almost musical.

It is the sound of a flute.

As he continued, Shem noticed how quiet and still the animals were. The music seemed to have a tranquilizing effect on them. Most of them seemed to be listening to the music with their eyes closed.

Shem finally spotted his father leaning back in the straw near a storage room blowing his flute. Not wanting the music to stop, Shem waved and backed away. He would look for leaks at the other end.

A short time later, sitting on a wooden beam, Shem dabbed a spot near his feet with pitch. As he reached to dab it again, the whole deck tilted to one side and then to the other.

Something scraped, then thudded against the outside of the ark beneath him.

The animals in the stalls near him stirred.

What?

He stood and started to move, but the floor of the deck in front of him seemed to rise to meet his step. He toppled forward and lost his grip on the container. The pitch spewed across the deck. He pushed himself up again but remained bent over, using his hands to steady himself against the beam as the deck tilted again.

The water must be lifting the ark from the platform.

He watched the motion of the deck and then took a few steps as the deck slanted down. He stopped and braced himself when the deck rose. He quickly stepped again on the downward motion and braced on the upward. By this method, he was able to make his way to the ramp.

Voices came from the deck above.

Sounds like...arguing?

The deck tilted as Temani bounded down the ramp, crashed into the wall, and tumbled to the floor at Shem's feet.

Japheth appeared at the top of the ramp. "Temani!"

Shem bent down to help Temani as Japheth, arms askew, maneuvered his way to the bottom.

Jazel and Gaddi, holding on to each other, shuffled after him.

Temani threw herself against the ramp-door. "Please, open the door," she cried.

Japheth reached his wife. "The door is sealed." He put his arms around Temani and held her tight.

"But, my family is out there. I hear them knocking on the outside of the walls."

Japheth stroked her hair. "Temani, you are hearing the sound of tree trunks from the platform bumping up against the ark. The water is too deep for anyone to be out there."

"No-o-o-o!" She pressed her head against his chest and sobbed.

Jazel and Gaddi, each with tear-stained cheeks, positioned themselves on both sides of Temani. Japheth released her into their care. They put their arms around her and the three of them slowly ascended the ramp.

Japheth shook his head. "She thinks her family is..."

Shem nodded. "I know...I know."

After Japheth followed the women up to the next deck, Shem stood still and listened. *Tree trunks?*

***

Shem staggered into the eating area. The floor, still swaying, was littered with bowls, utensils, vegetables, and fruits that toppled off shelves and tables. Ham sat at the eating table with his head down on his arms.

Shem clutched the edge of the table and lowered himself down onto a stool next to him.

"How can you sleep at a time like this?"

Ham slowly raised his head. "I am not sleeping. This constant movement is making me sick." He lowered his head back onto his arms.

Jazel, Gaddi, and Temani emerged from Temani and Japheth's room. With heads lowered, they silently shuffled over to the table. Jazel plopped onto a stool next to Shem. Gaddi stood behind Ham and softly stroked his hair. Temani sat next to Jazel and leaned her head on her shoulder.

Noah and Henna entered arm in arm, each seemed to be holding the other up. Henna immediately bent down to pick up a bowl from the floor.

"Do not worry about that now." Noah pulled her back upright. "Come. Everyone, sit at the table. The stools are sturdy. We need to be together and talk about what is happening. Where is Japheth?"

The sound of sandals shuffling turned faces toward the entrance to the room. Japheth appeared in the doorway looking somber.

"Here I am. I...I was looking out the gap we left at the top of the wall." He looked directly at Temani. "I saw only water."

As Japheth took a stool and scooted next to Temani, Noah scanned the faces at the table.

"I know this is a terrible and sad day for Gaddi, Temani, and Jazel. I am sorry for the loss of your families. I know you loved them. I know Yahweh loved them as well."

Temani wiped her eyes. "How can you say that?"

Noah placed a hand over his heart. "I know because he impressed it upon my heart, long before you all were born, to confront them time and time again, asking them to turn from their own ways and follow him. Yes, Yahweh is compassionate and grieves with us."

Shem knew his father was right. His father had confronted the people as long as he could remember. If Yahweh did not love the people, he would not have asked his father to do it.

Noah continued. "But remember, Yahweh is also holy and must hold his people accountable for their wickedness. This is the day Yahweh had decreed a long time ago to judge the people he created. He revealed it to my father in a dream when he was a young man."

Jazel perked her head up. "The dream about the seeds and the jewel in a wooden bowl."

"Yes. The elders used to speak of a future judgment when I was a child, but as the seasons passed, and the elders went the way of the First Man, only my father would speak of it."

Shem nudged Ham, still with his head down on the table. "He told us so many times before we went to sleep, we could retell the whole dream word for word."

Noah pointed at Shem. "That is exactly why he did it. So you all would know it by heart."

Japheth nodded. "Knowing the dream was the key factor for me to believe when you told us to build this ark."

"Since you all were little, Yahweh had prompted me to confront the people of our village with their evilness."

Ham lifted his head. "Not only the village. You confronted us too." He lowered his head back onto the table.

"Yes, and you can be glad now that I did. Yahweh is showing us mercy as he is judging his people. Judgment by the living God, as you can see, can be a terrifying thing. But in this ark, we are passing over his judgment."

"Just like the bowl in the dream," Jazel said.

"We did not know when we were learning grandfather's dream," said Shem, "that we would be the eight seeds in the bowl."

Two tiny birds flew into the room and lit on a shelf.

Noah laughed. "We, and our animal guests here. We will all start over again, no longer to be criticized or shunned when trying to live according to the ways of Yahweh. We will make a new world, starting fresh, without evil at every turn."

The deck tilted dramatically to one side. They all grasped the edge of the table until it righted. Ham bolted from his chair and lunged through the opening.

Shem was thankful for the noise of the rain drowning out Ham's suffering.

Jazel frowned. "But remember the jewel? The jewel broke into eight pieces and they were planted with each of the eight seeds after the judgment. You said the jewel is a reminder to us that we all carry within us a nature that is prone to disobey Yahweh. Will not our new world eventually become the same as the old one?"

Shem shook his head in amazement. "That is a good question."

Noah scratched his beard. "No, not necessarily. The knowledge of our disobedient nature had been hidden all this time. But, now it has been revealed to all of us. If we keep this knowledge fresh in the minds of our children, and our children's children, then they will understand and will not be deceived by their evil urges."

Shem shrugged. "I do not know, Father. Sometimes, it was only the fear of having to face you that kept me from being disobedient. Jazel has a point. There has to be more to keeping our new world from reverting to the old ways."

Japheth shifted on his stool. "Facing the judgment of Yahweh is more terrifying than facing Father's. Maybe after this flood, the fear of Yahweh will be greater than their urges."

Ham staggered into the room and lay his head back onto the table. Gaddi rubbed his shoulders.

Noah frowned, then smiled. "My father insisted that Yahweh loves us so much that he will not let it get that bad again. At the right time, he will devise a way to remove the disobedient nature from us and restore to us the relationship the First Man had with him before his disobedience."

Jazel leaned her head back against Shem. "I wonder what it was like in the Garden of Eden before..."

Gaddi giggled. "Ham says that no one wore clothes in the beginning."

Without lifting his head, Ham waved an arm toward his wife. "Gaddi, please."

"It is true," Noah said, as he placed his hand on Henna's. "There was no reason to hide, no shame to feel, no thoughts to be embarrassed about. Adam and Eve took joy in Yahweh's presence…and Yahweh delighted in his closeness with them."

Jazel nuzzled closer to Shem. "Like a marriage? Do you really think Yahweh loves us that much?"

Noah spread his arms wide. "Look around you. The land is covered with water, but we are safe and secure in this ark. Thanks be to Yahweh."

No one spoke.

Noah yawned and then helped Henna up off her stool. "I have lost track of how long of a day it has been. But I know morning will come sooner than we wish. Your mother and I are going to our room. If you are not exhausted enough, you can clean up in here. Otherwise, it can be left until morning."

As though it were contagious, everyone at the table began yawning.

Shem felt his eyelids become heavy. "Tomorrow sounds like a better time to clean. I will go and take delight in my closeness to my pillow."

He put his arm around Jazel and the two of them slowly shuffled to their room.

Chapter 14

Shem ambled out of the living area toward the ramp. He spotted Ham sitting atop a beam near the ceiling gazing out one of the windows at the top of the wall.

"Did you see two large red, yellow, and blue birds fly through here?"

Ham shrugged. "It has been moons since the rain stopped. How much longer do we have to float in this water?"

Shem smiled. "You are still not accustomed to our ever-moving floor?"

Ham leaned his head against the frame of the window. "I want to stand on solid ground again--feel the heat on my face from my forge and swing my hammer against red-hot metal."

Shem laughed. "You remind me of my oxen down on the lower level confined to their small stall. I think they long to dig their hooves into the dirt and pull against the yoke."

Ham frowned, slid off the beam, and dropped to the deck. He faced Shem and narrowed his eyes. "I think Yahweh has forgotten about us."

Two large, brightly colored birds flew past them, cawing loudly.

"How could he forget about us with all the noise these birds make?"

Ham drew in a breath. "You think this is all a joke?" He shoved past Shem, bumping Shem's shoulder, then stomped off toward the living quarters.

Shem shook his head. He wanted to be mad at him, but he also had recently entertained similar thoughts about Yahweh's memory. He decided to return to the bird area where he had left Jazel.

Jazel, sitting on a sack of wheat, held a handful of seeds out to a colorful group of birds.

She giggled as the birds carefully picked the seeds from her hand and cracked them open with their sharp beaks. "Your bird-friends returned without you a little while ago. I thought you must have gotten lost."

Shem slowly moved closer, careful not to disturb the birds, and sat on the floor beside her. "I ran into Ham."

Jazel rolled her eyes. "Let me guess. He was perched up on a beam near the window."

"Just like one of your birds, except his chirping grates on your ears like the cawing of my bird-friends over there." He pointed to a couple brightly adorned birds, who were eyeing them from a nearby branch.

Jazel shook the remaining seeds from her hand, shooing the birds away. "He has never adjusted to living on the ark. Gaddi has complained more than once about his grumblings. What is it this time?"

Shem helped her up. "He thinks Yahweh has forgotten about us."

"Forgotten?" Jazel laughed. "I think Yahweh has given us a rest from our labors. We have never had it so good. I have not once seen you work up a sweat feeding the few animals that are not sleeping. The four of us women take turns preparing and cooking meals. We have more family time than ever before." She put her arms around him and squeezed. "And, you are never more than three hundred cubits away from me. What more can you want?"

Solid ground came to his mind, but he knew agreeing with her was the wiser answer. "I cannot think of anything better." He patted her on the rear. "Let us go find some of this *family time* you desire."

***

In the eating area, Shem and Jazel found Ham, sitting at one end of the table watching his father and Japheth arm wrestling at the other end.

Japheth, red faced and grimacing hard, struggled to keep his wrist from touching the table. Noah appeared cool and calm. He glanced up at Shem and smiled.

Shem sat on a stool next to Ham, while Jazel sat across from him.

"I can tell how this is going to end," Shem said.

Ham showed no emotion. "The way it always ends."

Thump.

"Aaarrgh!" Japheth collapsed onto the table.

"Boys." Henna called from the connecting preparation room. She shushed Temani, and Gaddi, who giggled behind her. "Your father still thinks he is as young as his children. I will never hear the end of it unless one of you can show him his age."

Japheth massaged his arm. "Shem. You are stronger than me. You show Father how old he is."

Shaking his head, Shem turned to Ham. "If anyone can show him his age, it will be Ham. He has arms like an ox from swinging a hammer all day."

Ham shrugged. "I have not swung a hammer since coming aboard the ark. But, how can I let a chance pass to show Father his age?"

Noah laughed. "You swing a hammer, and I work a saw. We shall see which produces a stronger arm."

Ham got up and took Japheth's place on a stool across from his father. The women came out from the other room and stood at the end of the table.

Shem studied his father's face, but it did not betray any nervousness. Ham was as calm as he had ever seen him. Each of them gripped the other's hand.

Shem put a hand on top of theirs. "I will tell you when to start."

The two men adjusted their grips and took deep breaths, each looking into the eyes of the other.

The room became quiet.

"Ready?" Shem said.

The men nodded.

Shem removed his hand. "Go!"

Immediately, the muscles on both arms became more defined. Noah's arm began to move slightly backward.

"Is that all you have?" Noah gritted between clenched teeth.

Ham grunted. "I am saving the best until last."

Just then, a low scraping sound rumbled from below, and the rhythm of the deck's swaying halted briefly. The deck rose again, another scraping sound, and then it lowered and stopped with a thud. This time the deck remained still, but at a slight tilt.

Everyone stood motionless, waiting for another movement, or another sound.

Ham released his grip. "It is not moving. The deck is not moving."

For the first time since they boarded the ark, Shem saw his brother laugh.

Ham jumped up and grabbed Gaddi's arms. "We are on the ground. We are on the ground." He sang it like a song. "No more up and down. We are finally on the ground."

Jazel looked at Noah. "Is it true? Are we on the ground?"

Noah raised his brows. "It appears so."

Shem took Jazel by her arms and swung her around. "Yes, I think we *are* on the ground. Ham, run to your perch and see if you can see any land."

Ham broke from his embrace of Gaddi and sprinted out of the room. Shem and the others followed. Ham quickly pulled himself up onto the beam and stuck his head out the small window. He craned his neck to scan the horizon.

"Well?" Japheth said.

Gaddi raised her voice. "What do you see?"

He slowly pulled his head back in. "Nothing."

"What?" several yelled.

Ham dropped from the beam and looked directly at his father.

"There is a thick mist hanging over the water. It is hard to see passed it. I do not see any land...just water."

Noah ran toward the bird area.

"Where are you going?" Henna asked.

"I will be right back," he said as he disappeared through an opening.

Shem and the others waited under the window. In just a short while, Noah returned with something dark in his hands.

"Follow me," he said as he continued past them.

Jazel pulled on Shem's tunic. "Where are we going?"

Shem raised his shoulders and then followed behind the others.

Noah led them to a ladder mounted against the wall leading to a trap door on the ceiling. He cradled a medium sized black bird in one arm and pulled himself up the ladder with the other. He opened the door, letting it fall open against the outside roof. Fresh air blew in through the open hatch.

Shem put a foot on the first rung of the ladder and lifted his head to face the breeze. "We could use more of this." His brothers pressed against him on the ladder.

Noah raised the bird up through the opening and tossed it skyward. The bird flapped its wings, cawed, and then disappeared out of sight.

Noah blocked the sun from his eyes. "This mist only gives you a limited view. If there is land near, this raven will find it and roost."

They waited, and in a short while, they heard the familiar cawing.

Noah poked his head up through the opening. "The raven is roosting on the roof of the ark." He lowered his head back through the hatch door, descended the ladder, and surveyed all the sad faces. "We will wait a few days and then try this again."

Ham muttered as he slumped past Shem. "Stuck in the middle of nowhere."

Chapter 15

Jazel laughed as the small hairy beast she had been feeding a banana curled back its lips and flashed a giant smile, as though it was thanking her for the food. It then leaped against the wall, pushed off with its feet, reached up to a wooden rafter with one arm, and swung itself up into a sitting position atop it.

She turned to Shem, who was tossing cobs of corn to four-footed animals in another pen. "Do you wish you could do that?"

"To do that, I would need another cubit's length on each arm."

"Shem." A voice full of urgency called from the direction of the ramps.

Shem dropped the sack of cobs at Jazel's feet. "Sounds like Japheth. Could you watch these cobs?" He did not wait for her answer, and immediately headed toward the call.

Making his way past the stalls, Shem saw Japheth, Ham, and his father disappear up the ramp. He jogged the final distance and caught a glimpse of them going up the ramp on the next deck up. It looked like his father had a bundle in his hands.

By the time Shem made it to the top deck, his brothers were waiting at the bottom of the wall-mounted ladder beneath the hinged door on the roof. His father, at the top of the ladder, pushed the hatch open. A shaft of light enveloped him as he pulled his way up through the hatch.

A little out of breath, Shem approached his brothers. "Are you releasing another bird?"

"Yes," Japheth said. "Father believes that flatter land cannot be too far away."

Shem felt tingles in his stomach. He watched Ham then Japheth ascend the ladder and disappear through the light. He followed Japheth and poked his head through the opening. A crisp wind immediately smacked him in the face.

Shem crawled onto the deck afraid to stand until his eyes could adjust to the light. He inhaled the cool air deep into his lungs. It exhilarated his senses. A faint humming sound came to his ears. He blinked until his eyes finally could see clearly. Giant waves exploded against rocks just below the ark spraying foam high into the air.

Shem looked beyond the breakers and took in a breath. Above a thin mist a peak of land could be seen in the distance protruding above the water level.

It seemed to him that dry ground reached from the bottom of it to most of the way toward the ark. Shem pivoted and found that another peak, just as tall, rose above the water on the opposite side of the ark. Dry land extended from that peak toward the ark as well.

His father reached into a pouch and released the dove into the air. It circled the ark and then flew out of sight toward one of the peaks. It had been seven days since the they released the raven and after a couple days, they had not seen it again.

I do not see any trees on those peaks. I hope Father is right about flatter land being near.

Shem tried to look confident and smiled at his brothers. Japheth returned the smile, a little forced probably, but Ham made no pretenses. His face showed no emotion, but his eyes betrayed a hint of hope.

The four of them re-entered the ark and waited at the bottom of the ladder in silence until it became obvious the dove must have found a place to land.

"Well," Noah said. "I think I will get back to repairing that wobbly table leg. It does not take four of us to watch for the dove's return."

The three brothers looked at each other.

Ham folded his arms and leaned against the wall. "I will wait for the dove."

Japheth excused himself. "I have lower level chores to do. Let me know when the dove returns."

Shem nodded at Ham. "I left Jazel by herself feeding the animals. I will check on you later."

He returned to the ramp and descended to the deck below. He found Jazel carrying her hairy friend around on her hip as she tossed corn cobs to a couple curly-tailed pigs.

He approached her from behind and patted the contented adoptee on the head. "So, we have a new baby?"

Jazel swung around. "I wish." Her eyes sparkled.

"Maybe Yahweh will grant that wish when we get off this ark."

"Yes," a slight smile curled the edges of her lips. "We have a forest to grow with parts of your grandfather's jewels inside." She let her friend down from her hip and leaned into her husband.

He pulled her close and gave her a passionate kiss. "I think I am going to like our new world."

***

Later that afternoon, the women were all giggles as they prepared the evening meal. Shem, Japheth, and Ham sat at the table inspecting one of the legs of the table. Shem lowered himself to one knee and looked at the underside, where the leg connected to the top.

Ham put his hands on the corner of the table and pressed against it. "Father repaired the leg."

Japheth laughed. "At least he put *his* day to good use."

Ham shrugged. "I waited all afternoon at the bottom of that ladder—no dove. Are we never getting off this ark?"

Noah strutted into the room holding one hand high. "Do not be so quick in giving up."

"What is that?" Japheth asked.

Noah held out his hand to reveal a small twig with a couple leaves on it. "This is an olive branch. Our dove just returned with it in its beak. This means there are trees above the water that will soon have fruit."

Ham broke a smile across his face. "Does that mean we can leave the ark?"

"Soon, son. I know waiting for Yahweh is hard, but when the time is right, he will let us know."

Shem wandered into the preparation room and put an arm around Jazel's shoulder as she stirred a pot of savory beans over the fire. "Soon we will have a home to start that forest you wished for."

She leaned into him. "Home or ark, I am happy."

Shem looked around the room. He watched his mother, Temani, and Gaddi working together to prepare a meal for his father and brothers, who sat at the table talking about what the new world will look like.

He could not remember his family being so close since he was a child. Maybe life in the new world will be different than before.

"I am happy too."

***

Shem stood atop a ladder leaning against the wall next to the huge door of the ark. Ham stood atop a different ladder leaning against the wall on the other side of the door. They each wedged a metal bar Ham had forged into the space between the door and the frame. The hot water they had been pouring into this space had softened the pitch used to seal it shut so many moons earlier. Noah, Japheth, and the four women held on to a rope that ran up to the ceiling, over a rafter, and threaded an eye in a beam at the top of the door.

"Hold tight to the rope," Shem called down to the two on the deck. "When we free the door, it will pull the rope. Hold it in position before lowering it until Ham and I can get down there to help hold the weight."

"We have it," Noah said.

Shem looked over at Ham. Ham nodded.

"Here we go," Shem said.

Shem pulled hard on his bar. This door had held firmly against a torrent of water and debris without so much as a small leak.

There were no spikes, no locks, holding this door in place. Yahweh alone had secured it. What would it take to open it?

Surprisingly, the door moved easily away from the frame. He and Ham connected eyes briefly, and then quickly descended the ladders and joined the others on the rope.

"Let it out slowly," Noah yelled. "Hand over hand, so you will not burn your hands."

As the rope slid through Shem's hands, and the door began to lower, light flooded into his eyes. It was so bright, that, even squinting he could not see past his father. It was not until the rope became slack, that he realized the door was on the ground.

He dropped the rope and held his hands up in front of his face. "The sun is too bright."

The eight of them stood motionless.

"I waited a long time for this." Ham pushed past Japheth and his father. "I cannot wait any longer."

Ham, with hands blocking the sun, walked down the door ramp, and placed his sandaled feet on dry ground. "It is as firm as before," he yelled back to the others. "We are home!"

The others laughed and followed him to the bottom of the ramp. Shem's eyes, tearing from the glare, finally began adjusting to the brightness. Was the sun brighter, or had they been inside so long it just seemed brighter? And the air, so fresh and cool.

Shem breathed in deeply. He felt invigorated. He held out his hand. "Go for a walk?"

Jazel smiled and took his hand. They walked a short distance from the ark to survey their surroundings.

The ark seemed to be nestled on a small plateau between two mountainous peaks. The soil was more rocky than fertile.

A short walk in one direction and they could see that the land below them was sparse with trees and descended quite rapidly down to the water level, probably as far below them as the peaks rising above them.

"I had always envisioned dismantling the ark and using the wood to build our homes," he said. "But these new surroundings do not lend themselves to farming or raising goats."

Jazel leaned her head on his shoulder. "What will we do?"

Shem led Jazel back toward the ark. "I am sure Father will know the answer to that question."

They returned to the ark, and the others, slowly wandering back as well, seemed to have come to the same conclusion.

Ham, not as happy as when he first stepped on ground, asked, "Father, what are we going to do? We cannot live here."

Noah's eyes sparkled.

"The first thing we are going to do is let our guests loose so they can multiply and fill our new world."

"But, Father—"

"No. First things first. Yahweh has spoken."

Seeing his brother's faces, Shem felt as though he was not the only one who wished Yahweh would speak louder so all of them could hear.

Jazel tugged on Shem's cloak. "Come on. They have been cooped up as long as we have, and in smaller areas. It will be hard, though, to say goodbye to some of them. We have become so close."

Soon, as the stalls were opened, the animals seemed to come alive. Shem had to yell to be heard above the hooting and cawing, and the growling and grunting. Unlike their calm entry into the ark, their exit seemed chaotic and even nervous. The various cats squatted low and darted between the legs of the larger animals. Most of the animal's flinched at Shem's touch, backing or scrambling out of his reach.

Jazel came running along the wall. Tears streaked her face.

Shem took her by the arms and searched her face. "What is it?"

She drew a breath. "My hairy friends run from me, as though they are afraid of me. My birds will not acknowledge me either. What happened to them?"

Shem shook his head. "Let us go outside."

Shem and Jazel made their way down the ramp and joined the others a short distance away.

"They seem calmer when we distance ourselves from them," Japheth said.

Temani pointed toward the slope. "Most of them are heading down to the water."

Shem's eyes surveyed the exodus. "Have you seen my oxen?"

"They do not seem to want to leave," Ham said. "They were still in their stall when I left."

Noah stepped forward and said, "Come with me and gather stones. We must build an altar to Yahweh. Remember, he took us over the judgment of all mankind, and set us down safely in this new world."

Shem nodded. He knew that it was only by Yahweh's grace and mercy that they were still alive. In no time at all, they had built an altar, and Noah sacrificed burnt offerings on it for their thankfulness. After the offerings were consumed, the air around them seemed to still.

"Be fruitful and increase in number, and fill the earth," boomed a voice.

Shem heard the voice but saw no one speaking. It was as though it came from inside his head. He glanced at the others. All but his father had astonishment across their faces. His father had closed eyes and a slight smile.

"The fear and dread of you has fallen on all the beasts of the earth and all the birds of the air, upon every creature that moves along the ground, and upon all the fish in the sea."

Shem caught Jazel's eye.

"Everything that lives and moves will be food for you. Just as I gave you the green plants, I now give you everything."

Shem listened as Yahweh talked directly to them all about being accountable for the lives of others. He established a covenant with them, promising never again to destroy the earth with a flood. He also put a sign in the sky, a colorful rainbow, to remind them of his promise.

Yahweh's words were powerful, yet, soothing to his soul. He did not want them to stop. When they did, he yearned to hear more. He waited, it seemed like forever, before he heard his father speak.

"Let us go back into the ark and discuss what is next while we eat."

No one responded verbally, but everyone slowly moved toward the ark. Shem, still amazed at hearing Yahweh's voice, now understood why his father had continuously confronted the people with their rebelliousness, and pleaded with them to return to Yahweh, even to the very end.

I wonder if I will ever hear Yahweh's voice again.

Chapter 16

The chatter at the table was almost pure excitement. Noah stood and raised his hands to hush them. "You have heard from Yahweh. May he now direct your lives in the new world as he has directed mine. Tomorrow we will leave the ark."

"Yes!" Ham shouted.

Shem could not help laughing with the others.

Noah continued. "Gather what you can carry, and we will follow the water as it lowers. Bring the seeds we stored for planting and the few sheep and goats. Don't forget your tools. Shem, load your oxen with as much as you can."

A few days later, the eight of them packed their essentials and left the ark. They descended the steep terrain to camp down near the water.

Shem noticed that the water had lowered considerably since they had emerged from the ark. The descending water revealed that the ark was resting high on a ridge stretching between what was becoming a towering mountainous peak and a secondary lower peak.

He had thought they would eventually return and salvage the wood from the ark to construct their homes, but as the ocean level continued to lower, he soon realized the distance back to the ark would be too much to haul timber. His father seemed to come to the same conclusion.

Noah strained to locate the ark far above him on the mountain. "Ham, you and Japheth come with me back to the ark to carry your forge down here. We want it to stay close enough to retrieve when we get to the bottom of this mountain. Shem, you wait here and watch over things until we return."

"I will bring one of my bee-hives also," said Japheth as he and Ham started back up with their father.

Shem called after them. "Just keep your bees a distance from where we are camping." He joined Jazel sitting on a large rock overlooking the women down at the water's edge washing their feet.

Jazel leaned against him. "I do not see any other land above water in this direction. This mountain must be a very high mountain."

Shem put his arm around her and squeezed. "More land will emerge soon. I was glad Father went back for the forge. We will need it to make tools to build our new dwellings."

Jazel took one of his hands and placed it on her tummy. "When you build our new dwelling, we will need an extra room next to ours."

"Wha...what do you mean?" Shem looked down at his hand and then up at the smile on her face. "Are you...are we going to..."

Jazel nodded. "I was waiting for the right time to tell you."

Shem could not contain the explosion of happiness inside him. He yelled down to the women. "Jazel is with child! We are having a baby!"

***

They continued their downward trek, camping and moving their supplies lower, camping and moving their supplies lower. It became a pattern they followed until finally, the ocean retreated below the mountain and revealed a flat fertile plain as far as the eye could see. They named the plain Shinar, as two magnificent rivers flowed away from the mountain and ran clear to the horizon.

At the base of the mountain, the men built temporary shelters while the women arranged a food preparation and eating area.

Soon, a sense of normalcy brought peace to Shem as he focused on building his new home for Jazel and the coming baby.

It did not take long to discover that in the rich soil, Noah's grapes grew abundantly, as did everything they planted. The forest covering the lower slopes of the mountain quickly regained their splendor and provided ample timber.

Shem was impressed with this new world. Everything seemed more colorful. The sun burned brighter and hotter mid-day. In the evenings, he had never seen so many stars, and the moon seemed twice as bright.

One day, as he worked on the roof of their new dwelling, he watched dark clouds form in the sky. It felt very similar to the day Yahweh brought the flood. Rain began to fall.

Jazel came to the doorway. "Shem?"

He heard the fear in her voice and jumped down from the roof. He took Jazel's hand. "Come. Let us find Father."

At his father's dwelling, the others were gathered under his roof watching the rain. From the look on their faces, he and Jazel were not the only ones reliving that day in their minds.

"Do not fear," his father said. "Remember, Yahweh said there would be more rain. And that he would put a bow in the sky to reassure us of his covenant not to flood the earth again."

"I do not see any *bow* in these clouds," Ham mumbled.

"Be patient, my son."

Shem searched the skies. It seemed a little lighter off to the west. A short time later the rain lessened. Some of the clouds seemed to spread apart and beams of sunlight shot through to the ground.

"Look!" cried Japheth. He pointed toward the beams of sunlight.

An arc of multiple colors spread across the sky.

"Look at all the colors!" Gaddi exclaimed.

Jazel tightened her grip on Shem's arm. "I have never seen anything so beautiful."

"Is that Yahweh's bow?" Temani asked.

Noah stepped outside. "That is the sign of Yahweh's covenant with us. We do not have to be fearful. Yahweh has promised a future for us."

Shem mused. *A bright and colorful future.*

***

Shem lashed the last of the beams to the roof when he heard Jazel's cry from out in front of the dwelling.

"Shem!"

Shem jumped down from the roof and ran to Jazel.

Jazel held the lower part of her enlarged stomach with one hand as she reached for Shem's arm with the other. The ground was wet at her feet.

Through clenched teeth, she managed to squeak out, "It is time."

Shem's eyes darted around. He scooped Jazel up and carried her into their dwelling and placed her on their bed.

He watched her hands rubbing her stomach. The pain seemed to have subsided. "How can I help? What do I do?"

Jazel managed a quick smile. "Run and get your mother, Temani, and Gaddi. I want them here when the pain returns."

Shem could not get out the door fast enough.

When the women arrived, Temani and Gaddi disappeared into the sleeping room. Henna pushed Shem outside. "Start a fire and heat a cauldron of water. Go quickly."

Shem rushed to the firepit, glad to be doing something productive. Soon, his father and brothers arrived. They sat and chatted, stoking the fire, watching Shem, and keeping an eye on the door of the dwelling.

Soon, Gaddi appeared in the doorway with an empty pot. "Fill this with hot water."

Shem jumped up and took the pot. Ham swung the arm holding the cauldron away from the fire. Shem filled the pot and handed it to Gaddi, keeping hold of it until Gaddi looked him in the eyes.

"She is doing fine." She pulled the pot away and disappeared back into the dwelling.

Shem shrugged and slumped back to the fire.

Not long after that a scream pierced through the window opening.

Shem jumped up and ran into the dwelling, only to be pushed back outside by the women.

Noah laughed. "It is hard becoming a father, because we cannot do anything to quicken the birth or make it less painful."

Shem heard a baby's cry.

Before Shem could react, Temani opened the door and announced, "It is a boy!"

Shem ran back into the house and stood in the doorway to their room. There, lying on Jazel's breast was a tiny pinkish baby. Jazel looked up at Shem and beckoned him closer.

"Meet your new son."

Chapter 17

Approximately 130 years later.

Meshech ducked just in time to avoid the fist swung at him. With head down, he lunged forward hitting the guard in the chest with the top of his head, pushing him hard into the wall behind him. The guard dropped to his knees and gasped for air.

Hul, the larger of the two, held the other guard from behind in a bear-hug. He lifted him up and slammed him down onto the stone floor on his side. The guard let loose of his spear and lay motionless.

"Let us make a run for the gate," cried Meshech.

Hul picked up the guard's spear. "I am right behind you."

They moved in the shadows close to the wall until they could see the gate.

Meshech stopped and scanned the area. "The gate is still open and only one guard."

He watched the guard briefly.

"I will distract the guard while you sneak up from behind."

Hul nodded and waited for his brother to approach the guard. While the guard questioned Meshech, Hul came up behind him. The guard spun around quickly catching Hul in the upper arm with the edge of his spear blade. But it was too late. Hul brought the handle of the spear he carried down hard across the face of the guard. The guard was out before he hit the ground.

The two men ran through the gate disappearing into the night.

***

While Jazel cleaned up in the preparation room after dinner, Shem stepped outside. He wandered behind their dwelling and sat on a bench under a huge acacia to watch the sun set after another hot afternoon. Across the plain of Shinar, vivid red, orange, and dark blue plumes of smoke rose from Ararat, silhouetted against the colorful sky. Even without the plumage, it was truly a majestic mountain towering above the plain. *How long had it been since the ark had come to rest on it?*

Jazel approached quietly from behind and placed her hands on Shem's shoulders and squeezed. "Are you at the mountain again?"

He patted the bench seat and Jazel joined him.

"I was just thinking," Shem said, "about our first days after coming down from the mountain. We thought life in our new world was going to be easy."

"Easy?" Jazel laughed. "I had just given birth to our first son when the ground shook, and the mountain exploded. I thought the whole thing would come down on top of us."

"At least it waited until after we harvested our crops."

"Still, it was very hot crossing the plain. We had never experienced summer heat before." Jazel said.

"I am glad I had just finished making the two carts so we could move our supplies by oxen."

"Yes, our supplies." Jazel rolled her eyes. "Ham needed the better part of one cart just for his forge and tools."

Shem glanced southward. "I miss Ham."

Jazel bumped her shoulder against his. "You miss arguing with him? You miss his continual bad attitudes?"

Shem smiled. "I have to admit, when he and his family moved south, it was a lot more peaceful around here."

"When your father and Japheth's family journeyed west to the cooler coastal lands, I think Ham had a hard time looking to you as the head of the clans."

She laid her head on his shoulder. "He made the right choice to separate himself and his families from your influence and future conflicts."

"Maybe so, but Ham has always needed someone to remind him that Yahweh has not created us to live apart from him.

"I worry that his lack of faith will have an impact on his descendants, specifically, Canaan and his sons, Sidon, Jebus, and Girgash. When I was around them, old memories of people from before the flood come to my mind."

Jazel slid off the bench, took hold of Shem's hands, knelt in front of him and looked up into his eyes. "We all heard Yahweh's voice after we got off the ark. Ham knows that Yahweh is real. He will not go against his ways, especially after all that time without solid ground under his feet."

"I know." Shem rose and paced back and forth under the tree. "But, we have labored with our children to make sure they knew about the First Man and the sin inside us that brought about the terrible judgment of Yahweh. We taught them songs about the ark and the animals, and Yahweh's love for us...I fear Ham has not made the same effort."

Jazel returned to the bench. "What are you worried about?"

"I have heard disturbing stories coming from across the plains. My father made it clear that he felt Ararat's explosions were Yahweh's not-so-subtle way of encouraging us to obey his command to go and "fill the earth" instead of staying near the mountain."

Jazel swept her hand across the darkening horizon. "We traveled for many days to put distance between us and that mountain."

Shem sat on the bench next to his wife. "Yes, we did. And because of that, we have had a beautiful sunset to watch each night." He pulled her close.

Jazel snuggled under his arm. "Then what is there to worry about? Let us enjoy the last of the sunset."

Shem kissed the top of Jazel's head and stared at the mountain. *If there is nothing to worry about, then why do I have this uneasy feeling? Something is wrong and I need to find out what it is.*

***

Days later, two of Shem's grandsons came to his door. Shem eyed Hul as Hul's brother, Meshech, spoke. Hul was larger than his brother, and although his eyes were surrounded with laugh lines, they showed pain as he winced from whatever wound was behind the soiled cloth bound around his upper arm.

"We had a confrontation." Meshech clenched his hands into fists and buffeted the air between them.

"Settle down Mesh." Hul put a hand on his brother's shoulder.

Shem could not hold back a slight smile curving on the edge of his lips. He knew Meshech was always prone to over-animate his emotions.

Shem took Hul's arm softly. "Come in and let Jazel attend to this." He turned and called to the cooking room. "Jazel, we have visitors."

Jazel came and instructed Hul and his brother to sit at the dinner table. She disappeared back into the cooking room briefly and reappeared with a bowl of water and a clean cloth.

Shem grabbed a stool and sat across from the men. "I heard that you went to Babylon. What was so confrontational that it resulted in fighting?"

"The people..." Meshech shrugged off Hul's hand. "The people are of one mind with their leaders. They are gathering a huge work force for some massive building project, and because we were strangers, they thought they could force us to be part of it."

Hul made a fist and ground it against the palm of his other hand. "We persuaded them that they did not need us."

When Meshech mentioned the building project, Shem felt a nervousness deep inside.

He had participated in a building project before and nothing had been the same since.

Shem leaned forward on his stool. "Tell me more."

Meshech exchanged glances with Hul. "We do not know much more. The people in Babylon have sworn allegiance to a Hamite warrior called Nimrod. Whatever Nimrod says, the people do."

Hul looked up from watching Jazel clean his wound. "Nimrod wants some sort of giant tower built. It must be a huge task because the entire city is bent on erecting it."

"A Hamite warrior?" Shem looked at Jazel. "Do we have any relatives in Babylon?"

Jazel raised her shoulders. "I do not know."

Meshech tapped Hul on his other shoulder. "Did not we see a son of Shelah living there with his family?"

"Yes," Hul looked up at the ceiling. "I think...Eber was his name."

Without breaking his gaze with Jazel, Shem said, "I need to go talk with this Nimrod."

Jazel shook her head. "Let us find Eber and talk with him first."

"Us?" Shem frowned. "You are staying here. I do not have a good feeling about this Nimrod."

Jazel opened her mouth to speak, then stopped. She smoothed a clean cloth over Hul's wound and tied it firmly. "Leave this cloth on for at least two more days."

Hul flexed his arm a couple times and then smiled at Jazel. "Shall I come back to have you look at it?"

"That will not be necessary." Jazel picked up the remnant of blood-stained cloth and the bowl of water and started back to the cooking room. "I will be on the way to visit a relative in Babylon."

Chapter 18

On the fourth day of traveling, Shem and Jazel stopped under a large acacia off to the side of the path near the river. The far-reaching branches cooled the air under the tree and offered relief from the heat. Previous travelers had matted the grass under the tree which provided a comfortable, thistle free, resting spot.

Shem removed his travel satchel, wiped the sweat from his brow, and sat cross-legged on the ground with his back to the tree's trunk. "I do not know how I let you talk me into allowing you come with me."

Jazel laughed as she opened the flap of her satchel at her side and pulled out a flattened date cake. She broke it in half, lowered herself beside him, and handed him one of the halves.

"I know you so well, I know where your weaknesses are."

Shem took a bite and tried not to smile. "This is a dangerous journey. Remember Hul's injury?"

"Hul's injury?" She raised both her hands high. "Remember the whole world flooded with water? I was with you through that. I will be with you through this also. Besides, all our children have grown up and left the dwelling. I have nothing to do if I do not take care of you."

Shaking his head, Shem realized he was not going to make any headway in this discussion. He swallowed the last of his date cake and leaned against the acacia trunk and closed his eyes.

Jazel snuggled against his shoulder and let out a sigh. "How much further to the city?"

"I think we should make it there by nightfall."

"Good," she said. "I have not been to a city since we went to visit your grandfather. I look forward to walking in the market place."

"Market place?" Shem fidgeted. "Do you remember that market place? You did not want to walk there."

Jazel raised her head. "That was before the flood. People are not that way anymore."

"Mmmmm."

She poked him in the side with her finger. "Shem. Do not be so glum."

"I am remembering Hul's injury again."

Without responding, Jazel lay her head back on Shem's shoulder.

The two lay there awhile and then Shem prodded Jazel and motioned toward the pathway. "If we want to make it there by dark, we need to get going."

They grabbed their satchels, pried themselves away from the cool of the acacia, and returned to the path.

***

Stars twinkled above the lights in the distance.

"Babylon." Shem said.

"Finally. It will be nice to talk to other people. We have not seen another soul in two days."

Two days? Shem peered intently at the lights ahead. *We should have passed people coming from the city traveling east. Something is not right.*

Campfires illuminated tents spread out in all directions. Shem caught aroma of various food cooking and put his hand on his stomach to quiet a rumbling. Laughter seemed to rise above the buzz of chatter. Under their feet, the hardened ground gave way to smooth stones.

Jazel reached down and touched the stones. "Shem, look what they did to the road."

Shem took Jazel's hand. "We need to find the city center and see if some family has room to let us rest for the night."

Jazel watched several families eating around campfires. "They seem friendly enough."

Soon, lit torches burned along the sides the stone road. Merchants called out from booths.

"Come and see something new!"

"I have a scarf just for you!"

"Sharp knives!"

Shem pulled Jazel close and quickened his pace, and then pulled up short.

"What is this?"

Twenty paces in front of them stood a set of huge double, wooden doors twice their height and wide enough for two carts to enter side-by-side. The doors were erected into a giant stone wall that disappeared into the darkness in both directions. Two burly men, both wearing animal fur cloaks and holding spears, stood in front of the doors.

Shem and Jazel looked at each other.

Jazel whispered, "Did Meshech and Hul mention a wall around the city?"

Shem stared at the two men. "No wall, no gate. But they did mention having to fight."

Jazel squeezed Shem's arm. "Maybe we should turn back."

Shem slid the strap off his shoulder and handed his satchel to Jazel. "I will talk to the men and see if they will let us in. You stay here."

He walked toward the men. They fidgeted and then pointed their spears in his direction.

"What do you want?" barked one of them.

Shem stopped and put the palm of his hands held out toward them. "My wife and I have come from a village on the plains. We are looking for lodging for the night."

"It is too late. The gate is closed." barked the other one. "You will have to find lodging outside the city."

Shem wanted to try reasoning with them, but the way they pointed their spears, he knew they were not about to change their minds.

"When will the gates be opened?"

"Sunrise," one of them replied gruffly. And with finality in his voice, "Do not come back until after sunrise."

I guess the conversation is over.

Shem returned to Jazel. "Come on." He put his arm around her. "Let us find a soft place to spend the night. We will come back in the morning and see what is on the other side of this wall."

They retraced their steps past the merchants, past the tents, to just beyond the glow of all the lights, and settled in the cover of darkness to rest for the night.

Since it seemed late, and they were wearied from the journey, they decided not to make a fire and to call it a day. Shem knew he should smooth the ground before laying out the blankets but elected to skip it and sleep around the bumps. Sleep came quickly for both.

***

Shem awoke from an unrestful night of shifting positions to fit around the bumps under their blanket.

"Hmmmmm," Jazel groaned next to him. "Is it finally morning?"

Shen rubbed the small of his back. "I thought the sun would never rise." He stood and stretched his arms high over his head. "Ahhhhhhh-awk. What is that?" He bent and shook Jazel's shoulder vigorously. "Jazel, get up and look at this."

Jazel got to her feet and steadied herself against Shem. "Oh, my."

Rising above the stone wall, towering above the city, stood a mountain of a structure. Shem had never seen a building so massive, so tall. Thoughts of the ark came to his mind. But this structure dwarfed the ark. Both he and Jazel stood gazing unable to speak.

Finally, Shem forced his body to move and grabbed Jazel's hand. "We need to get closer."

She pulled back her hand. "Wait...our blankets and satchels."

Shem felt his cheeks warm. "Oh...sorry."

After packing their belongings, they quickly made their way back to the stone road hardly taking their eyes off the structure. Continuing to the gate, the two doors stood wide open and a throng of people moved in and out of the opening without any men with spears stopping them. They joined the throng.

Shem surveyed the city streets. "Does it not remind you of a larger version of our town before the flood." He pointed to the two-story, block-and-plaster-walled buildings lining the streets.

Jazel cringed. "It gives me the same creepy feelings too."

They continued toward the towering structure. It seemed to grow as they moved closer. They could now see a multitude of workers moving about the exterior, carrying what looked like loads of mud bricks and wooden beams. The familiar smell of melted tar filled the air. Shem could hear the hammering and the shouting of commands. A web of ropes and pulleys raised supplies to workers on levels above.

Shem realized the structure's base was not square, but circular. It rose in levels, each level about the height of a dwelling. Windows and doors seemed to be spaced around the outside of each level with stone stairways rising at intervals to the next level above. He counted twelve levels and a partial level above that which they were still working on.

"What are you two doing?" barked a voice from behind.

Shem spun around and found himself confronted by two spear-carrying men in animal furs like the ones at the gate. They did not look happy.

"We were watching the people working on the...structure." Shem recalled the people that had gathered each day to watch them working on the ark.

"Where are you from?" one of them barked again. "Why are you not helping with the work?" He motioned with his spear at Jazel. "And why are you not with the women preparing food for the workers or carrying water?"

Shem pulled Jazel close. "We have just arrived from our village four days journey from the west."

"All visitors," one of the men spouted, "are required to spend time helping with the construction. Come with us."

They lowered their spears to about waist high and gestured with them toward the construction area. Jazel tightened her grip on Shem. When Shem hesitated, one of them prodded him with the tip of his spear.

"Move."

Shem stepped back. "Be careful with that!"

"Move!"

"Shem!" Jazel pulled on his arm. "We need to go with them."

He realized these men were not going to listen to reason. He would wait and find someone more in charge to speak with. He turned and, with Jazel in-arm, followed the spearman that walked ahead. The second man followed behind keeping his spear pointed toward Shem's back. He understood now why Meshech and Hul decided to fight their way out of Babylon. He glanced at Jazel.

I should have made her stay home.

Chapter 19

At the base of the structure, lines of men carrying mud bricks and wooden timbers ascended a maze of steps and stairways. Some steps led to open doorways, while others rose to the next level and disappeared. Shem shook his head and marveled at the organization of the work. Several men seemed to do nothing more than shout orders directing the carriers to various stairways.

The two spearmen delivered Shem and Jazel to one of the men shouting orders.

"Two more workers," the spearman exclaimed above the noise.

The man in charge quickly focused a set of keen eyes on the two of them. "Avala!" he shouted. A young woman emerged from the shadows of a doorway and stood, eyes down, slightly behind him.

He pointed at Jazel. "You, woman. Follow Avala to the women who prepare food. They will tell you what to do."

"Wait." Shem protested. "We are just visitors. We just" He felt a sharp pain in his back.

"All visitors must help with building the tower," the spearman behind him barked.

The man in charge betrayed a slight smile. "You must learn our ways quickly. It is less painful."

Bewilderment turned to anger inside Shem. "Leave my wife alone."

"Shem," Jazel caught his eye. "I will be fine. I know how to cook. We will find each other tonight. You know how to work with wood. Do what they say."

Shem rubbed his back while he watched Jazel follow the woman up some steps. He wanted to grab her and try outrunning the spearmen back to the gate. Just before she disappeared through a doorway, she turned, lowered her eyebrows, and pointed her finger at him. He felt like a child being warned by his mother to behave.

"So, you work with wood?" The man in charge brought Shem's attention back.

Shem burned a hole in him with his eyes. "Yes, my father and brothers and I once built a wooden boat 300 cubits long, 75 cubits wide, and 50 cubits high."

The spearmen behind him laughed.

For the first time, the man in charge did not look so in charge. He stroked his well-trimmed beard, cocked his head, and stared at Shem more out of one eye than both. He motioned with one arm to the two spearmen and barked, "You two. Leave us. Go back to your duties."

Shem watched the spearmen retreat out of sight. *Why did he send them away?*

Two workers trudged past carrying a large wooden beam. The man shouted, "Take that up to the top."

The now not-so-in-charge man's eyes darted about the area. He ordered Shem to follow him as he moved toward an archway.

Shem paused seeing no spearmen to prod him. *What is this about?*

The man stopped at the opening. "Come quickly," he ordered again.

Shem decided to follow him. On the other side of the arch was a walkway running along the perimeter of the structure. He followed the man to the edge of a small raised terrace out of the path of workmen carrying supplies. The man sat on the edge and motioned Shem to join him. Shem just stared at him.

The man's face softened, and a hint of a smile appeared. He patted the terrace next to him. "Sit."

Shem moved slowly to the terrace and sat a comfortable distance from the man.

"When I was a young boy," The man held his hand about waist high. "my father told me stories his father had told him of a giant boat, about the size you described, filled with animals, that floated over great flood waters and landed atop the great mountain that smokes."

Shem began to smile.

"Many years ago," the man continued, "my family decided to move west to the land near the great sea. I have not thought about these stories until now. What do you know about them?"

"What is your father's name?"

"My father is Riphath, son of Gomer. I am Bakta."

Shem laughed out loud. "Your grandfather, Gomer, was he the son of Japheth?"

The man's eyes widened. "Yes, how did you know?"

"I am Shem. Japheth is my brother. I knew all his children. Gomer was his first born."

Bakta stared at Shem. "Are the stories true? Did you really build a giant boat and fill it with animals?"

Shem chuckled. "Animals of every type. Animals with fur, feathers, scales, and horns. Some with all of those."

Bakta shook his head. "Then there really was a flood that floated a boat as high as the mountains?" Bakta raised both arms over his head.

Shem remembered the day the floodwaters came. "Bakta," he spoke directly. "I have come for a purpose."

Bakta dropped his hands slowly into his lap. "And what is that, Shem, brother of Japheth?"

"I have come to speak with Nimrod."

Bakta stood. "Nimrod!" He seemed visibly shaken. "Why do you wish to speak with...him?"

Shem looked up at the structure towering above him. "I have come to persuade him to stop building this...this..."

"Tower to the Heavens!" Bakta proclaimed.

"Tower to the Heavens?"

"That is what the people are calling it. It will be the greatest building in all the land."

Shem cocked his head. "Why are you building it?"

"Why?" Bakta spread his hands out. "To bring people to Babylon. People are already coming from all around to see it, and it is only half-way done. It will make Babylon's name great. Babylon will be the center of the world. Why would you want to stop the building?

"Bakta, do you know why your family moved west to the great sea?"

He shook his head. "I was young and did not listen well. I only know they wanted to be near the water."

"The water was only part of the reason." Shem gestured and waited until Bakta sat again. "After the flood, when my family stood again on dry ground, Yahweh spoke to us. He told us not to live at the base of the mountain, but to scatter our families across the land to inhabit the whole earth. That is why my parents and my brother, Japheth, and his families went away. That is mostly why my brother, Ham, took his family and journeyed south. This tower Nimrod is building will cause people to gather in one place. This would go against what Yahweh commanded."

"But Nimrod is a great hunter and a greater warrior and leader of men. Yahweh has blessed him. Maybe Yahweh has changed his mind?"

Shem thought about how long ago his grandfather dreamed of the flood and how short a time it has been since the flood. "I do not think Yahweh has changed his mind. I have a bad feeling about what is happening here. Where can I find Nimrod?"

Bakta rose quickly and scanned the area around them. "You do not want to confront Nimrod. He is a strong man with a strong will. He answers to no one. I have heard stories." He stole a glance over his shoulder. "Those who oppose him are never seen again."

"Bakta, calm down. I just want to talk with him. I am brother to his grandfather. I knew his father, Cush when he was a child. He will not hurt me."

Bakta stared at Shem and stroked his beard. "Maybe you are right. Every few days Nimrod comes to see the progress of the workers. He climbs to the very top of the tower and looks out over Babylon and the surrounding area. He did not come today, so he will probably come tomorrow, just after sunrise."

Shem nodded and then looked up. "I will talk to him tomorrow...at the very top of this structure."

"So be it," Bakta bowed his head. "May Yahweh grant you success." He pointed past Shem. "That walkway to the left will eventually lead you to a grand entrance on the right. Enter the structure and the aroma of food will lead you to your wife."

Shem raised a hand. "Thank you, my friend. You may want to reconsider your decision not to live near water. It is good to have family close."

Bakta returned a half smile.

***

Shem hurried down the pathway that skirted the tower. He could not resist looking up and marveling at the workmanship of the massive structure, how they integrated stone and mud bricks, with wooden beams. He understood why people would come to see it.

He finally came upon a huge doorway with ornately carved wooden trim. He entered and found himself in a large room filled with tables and stools.

And just as Bakta had said, he was met with the pleasing aroma of cooked food. Inhaling deeply, he guessed the food was being prepared in a room off to the right.

He slowly opened the door. Immediately, he felt warm air coming from a row of fire pits against one of the walls. Smoke from the pits rose to a slanted ceiling above and disappeared through an opening to the outside.

Women were everywhere, preparing various foods as they chatted. It reminded him of one of Japheth's bee-hives. The sound of their chatter felt as warm as the air, very much like in the ark when his mother, Jazel, Temani, and Gaddi were in the food preparation room before the evening meal.

Shem stepped into the room. The voices near him quieted. He scanned the faces but no Jazel. A woman approached carrying a big knife and just as big smile.

She looked him over. "Are you lost?"

"I am looking for my wife...Jazel?" He looked past the woman.

"Jazel? The new one?"

"Yes...the new one."

She turned and yelled out, "Jazel? You have a visitor."

Heads turned and the room became quiet.

"Shem," came a small voice from the other side of the room.

The chatter slowly resumed as Jazel made her way toward him.

"Your wife is remarkable." The woman with the knife said. "She talks as though she knows me. You are very fortunate to have her."

Shem glanced at the woman and then back at his wife. "Yes...I am...fortunate."

The woman backed away and hugged Jazel as she passed.

Jazel nestled up to Shem, put her arms around him, and squeezed. "I was worried about you."

"It seems I did not have to worry about you."

"Come." Jazel took his hand. "There is someone I want you to meet."

She led him across the room, past a multitude of eyes surveying him, and to a table covered in flour.

A woman bent over kneading bread dough stopped and wiped a strand of hair from her face.

She stood up straight and Shem could not help but notice the lower part of her stomach bulging with child.

Jazel placed her hand on the woman's shoulder. "This is Lebana, wife of Eber, son of our grandson, Shelah. He works with the men on the tower."

Shem nodded his head. "Meshech and Hul mentioned we had relatives living here."

Lebana took Jazel's hand. "Your wife has spoken of things long ago. It would be an honor to have you stay with us during your visit. Eber will be happy to see family again."

Shem looked at Jazel. She was nodding. "We are thankful for your generosity."

Lebana's eyes sparkled briefly and then shifted to troubled. "I need to put this dough in the oven or it will not be ready when the men come to eat."

She returned to her table and quickly separated the dough into two sections and placed them on a metal plate of some sort. She snatched up the plate and scurried across the room toward the oven.

"Shem," Jazel said. "I would like to stay here and help Lebana until after the men are fed. Could you find something to do until then?"

Shem recognized the look on Jazel's face. It was the same as when their daughters were with child. Although it had been a long time, he knew Lebana had awoken those motherly feelings in Jazel. He would honor them.

When Lebana returned, they arranged a place for him to meet with them after the meal and then go to their home.

Shem left them to prepare the meal and searched for a place away from any spearmen. He found a place in the shade of the wall that circled the city. He sat and rested his back against the cool blocks.

What a day this has been? I am glad we did not turn out like Meshech and Hul. But what about tomorrow? Nimrod cannot be as bad as Bakta makes him sound. Hmmm…He is a son of Ham. Maybe I should reconsider?

Chapter 20

Lebana held a bowl of sweet corn bread out to Shem. "Have another piece."

Shem patted his stomach. "If I eat another bite I will burst. Thank you for such a grand meal."

Jazel picked up Shem's empty plate. "I will help you clean."

"Oh no." Lebana protested. "Leave it until later. I want to hear more about the ark and the animals."

Eber leaned back on his stool. "Yes, as a child, I heard stories from our parents and grand-parents. My brothers and sisters and I even sang songs about Yahweh bringing a flood, but hearing it from you, I know now it was not just childish tales."

Shem was happy to hear his and Jazel's efforts to pass the story of the flood on to their descendants was successful. But sad that in just four generations the story was beginning to become thought of as a *childish tale.*

"Eber." Shem paused briefly. "In all the stories you heard, did you hear any about the acorns and the jewel?"

Eber shook his head.

Shem winked at Jazel. "Let me tell you a story greater than the ark and the flood."

Shem told about his grandfather's dream, his meeting with the First Man, and the real jewel of Yahweh's love for mankind, and his plan to remove their sinful nature and restore them to an eternal intimate relationship with him.

Lebana cried and hugged Jazel.

Eber lowered his head and cleared his throat. "Well, I will admit that sometimes it is a struggle to do the right thing."

Lebana wiped her eyes. "I have never heard anyone speak about Yahweh's love for us. I hope it is true."

Shem smiled. "We are all living proof of Yahweh's love. He could have destroyed us all in the flood."

Eber walked to the open window and gazed toward the tower.

"Removing our sinful nature? We have witnessed much sinful nature in our city. We thought Nimrod would change that."

"What do you mean?" Shem asked.

"Nimrod built this city and put a wall around it for our protection. He trains and organizes the men to hunt and supply the city with meat. There is no one hungry here. If anyone wants food, just go work on the tower and he feeds them."

Lebana spoke up. "And all us women who cook for the workers are allowed to take any extra food home. He is a great man, generous, and looks out for our welfare."

"I see," Shem said. "you think this tower he is building is a good thing?"

"Oh, yes," Eber declared. "We are blessed to have him as our leader."

Shem struggled with his thoughts. "It has been a long day and I have someone to see at first light."

Eber stood. "I will show you your sleeping room."

Jazel picked up a plate again. "Shem, I will help Lebana clean and then join you."

Shem nodded and then followed Eber.

Later, when Jazel slipped into bed, Shem, still awake, waited for her to settle, and then whispered, "I do not know what to do?"

She lay her head upon his chest. "What is wrong?"

"After speaking with Bakta this morning, I was so sure I was doing the right thing by confronting Nimrod and stopping him from finishing this tower. But now I see how he is helping the people, and how they esteem him."

"I remember when you were not sure if building the ark was the right thing to do also. Go and talk with Nimrod and see how you feel. Go to sleep and you will feel better tomorrow."

Shem took in a breath. "You are right." He hugged her, turned his back to her, and drew the cover up to his chin.

"Good night," she whispered.

He felt Jazel snuggle her backside against him. "Good night," he whispered back.

***

Early next morning, before sunrise, Shem made his way to the tower. A few workers milled about but no one seemed to notice him. It was not hard finding stairs leading to the next level. He ascended and found another set of stairs. He ascended three more levels before he stopped to catch his breath. He gazed over the building near the tower. He could see the wall with the gate at the entrance. It was still closed.

He climbed the next three levels a little slower and stopped to breathe again. The sun would be breaking over the plain any time now. He continued his ascent and finally came to a plateau with open-aired unfinished walls, piles of sand, and stacks of wooden beams.

He walked across the floor to the side facing the sunrise and placed both hands on a half-finished waist high wall. A hawk circled in the air below him.

Shem's mind immediately went to the ledge on the mountain overlooking their village before the flood. As a young boy, he had always enjoyed watching birds soaring below the ledge.

Shem inhaled the air in front of him. Even from this height the aroma of cooked vegetables reached him. He looked past the hawk, past the great wall around the city, past the tents outside the wall. He noticed a work area near a stream where mud was collected and put into forms to dry into bricks. He could just make out a row of smoldering forges where metal spikes and rods were made. He was amazed at all the planning that must have gone into building this.

Maybe he was wrong about this tower. Maybe Nimrod is good for the people. There is no one else who could organize so many people to work together to build such a great structure.

The sound of sandals slapping against stone came from behind him.

He spun around and faced a group of men. One of them was clad in a bright yellow ornate robe. The rest of them wore the animal fir tunics and carried spears. Something about the man in yellow was familiar to Shem.

"What is he doing up here?" barked the man in yellow pointing to Shem. "Get him out of here."

The spear carriers advanced toward him.

Shem cried out to the man in yellow. "Nimrod, son of Cush, son of Ham, son of Noah. I am here to speak with you."

The men with spears grabbed Shem's arms and began to pull him away from the wall. Shem stiffened to resist.

The man in yellow raised his hand. "Wait!"

Shem felt uneasy as the man's steely eyes looked him over.

"What do you know about Noah and Ham?" the man in yellow growled.

The sun's first rays appeared over the hills and lit up the Nimrod's yellow robe with its metal trappings.

Bardo? A shiver ran up Shem's spine. *How could he...*He fumbled for words.

"Speak, or be gone," the man barked again.

"I am Shem, son of Noah...brother to Ham."

The man waved his hand and the spearmen released their hold of Shem.

"What do you want, brother of Ham? What do you have to say to me that you would come alone to the top of my tower at sunrise?" Nimrod stepped over to the edge and took in the view. His voice softened. "There is no finer view anywhere."

More people appeared from the staircase carrying stools and a small table. Others brought food and drink and set about preparing the table for a meal.

Shem turned toward the view. "There was a time, not too long ago, that everything you see from this tower was under water, higher than those mountains in the distance."

Nimrod did not seem surprised. "My father spoke of this when I was a child. He told me his father helped build a great ark that carried his family, and two of every type of animal, on top of the waters. He called it Noah's Ark. My grandfather journeyed far away to the lands in the south before I was born, so I could not ask him about it. I have always thought of this story as...a child's tales." He waved his hand as if he was waving away an annoying insect.

Shem did not wish the story to be brushed aside so easily. "I helped your grandfather build that ark. Yahweh was grieved because all those he created had turned away from him."

"He decided to wipe everyone from the face of the earth, but chose to use our family to start over again. It is not a child's tale. I was on the ark as it floated on the waters."

Nimrod looked at Shem and then returned his gaze to the view. "I do not think this is what you came to tell me? Tell me and be quick about it. My people have prepared a morning meal for me."

Shem saw that many more people had emerged from below and appeared to be waiting for Nimrod's attention. He took in a breath.

"When the waters finally receded, and we were able to leave the ark, Yahweh told us to spread across the whole earth and populate it.

"Your grandfather took most of his family and journeyed south. My father and my brother, Japheth, journeyed west. My family has spread across the plains and to the east.

Now, you are building a great tower to make Babylon a great city where people will gather together instead of scattering across the lands. I do not think Yahweh will be pleased about this. You must stop building this tower."

"Stop building the tower?" Nimrod laughed out loud. Heads turned. "I will not stop building this tower." His voice grew loud and his eyes flashed. "I have fought man and beast, and no one has ever stopped me from doing what I wanted to do."

He turned and spoke to the crowd. "When I was a hunter, you people called me a great hunter before Yahweh. But it was not Yahweh that made me great. It was my strength, my cunning, my abilities. It was I who built this city with walls around it and made it and you people great." He turned his head up toward the sun and proclaimed into the air. "I feed my people and I protect my people. Not Yahweh. And it is I who have encouraged the people to build this great tower to the heavens to show that we are a great people unto ourselves."

Shem felt the air change around him as Nimrod stirred the crowd around him. The voice of Nimrod faded into the background and a voice spoke softly inside his head.

Shem instantly knew whose voice it was.

Chapter 21

"Shem."

The voice was a whisper, but it penetrated to the deepest part of his being. Time seemed to come to a stop. He knew Nimrod was yelling, but it was the whisper inside his head that captivated his attention.

"Shem. Do not be afraid. I have listened to Nimrod's words. He thinks he is wise and understands. But I will make his words like one who babbles. I will use this great tower he created for unity to be known for division. My people *will be* scattered over the earth. I am Yahweh, who speaks, and it comes to pass."

Nimrod's voice boomed again. "I am Nimrod, your protector and provider."

Behind him the crowd echoed "Nimrod!" "Nimrod!" "Nimrod!"

Nimrod turned and faced Shem. His face had become disfigured with anger and his eyes glared as if on fire. He lifted his hand and pointed straight at Shem.

The image of Bardo in the water raging as the door of the ark closed flashed in Shem's mind. *Yahweh, help me.*

Nimrod opened his mouth and shouted. But whatever came forth sounded like babble. The unified chanting from the crowd broke immediately into disjointed, unintelligible words. Nimrod looked at his spearmen and shouted again. Wide-eyed, they looked back and forth from one to another, but, remained still.

The crowd tried speaking to one another, but from the confusion on their faces, no one understood anyone. Very quickly, they resorted to shoving and shouting at one another. Nimrod continued to bark at the spearmen. They backed away, dropped their spears, and ran for the stairs. Nimrod turned to the crowd and yelled at them. The crowd became chaotic. Shouts turned to screams. People shoved past others to get to the stairs. Some fell onto the floor or against the tables, which overturned strewing food and drinks everywhere.

Shem took advantage of the chaos and hurried toward the closest stairs. He glanced back and saw Nimrod with arms waving, still barking.

Stepping behind a frantic woman, Shem started descending the stairs. Two levels down, he stepped out onto an empty balcony overlooking the city.

He watched workers far below fleeing in all directions, leaving mud blocks, wooden beams, tubs of tar, and ropes scattered on the ground. Others ran from their homes, leaving their doors wide open.

It seems Yahweh has confused the whole city. I better get back to Eber's and check on Jazel.

Shem re-entered the stairway. A woman pulled on his arm until she caught his eyes and spoke something unintelligible to him. The fear in her eyes told him everything he needed to know. He sadly shook his head. She released him and hurried ahead of him down the stairs. Once outside, people scattered, disappearing down streets and around corners. Soon, the streets were empty.

The sound of arguing, or was it crying, came from nearby. Shem crept up to an alcove and found Bakta shaking a young woman.

"Stop crying," Bakta commanded.

He held tightly to the young woman. It was the same young woman that led Jazel to the cooking room when they arrived. She shrieked uncontrollably.

"Bakta," Shem called out.

Bakta jerked, noticeably surprised, and lost his grip on Avala who fled past his grasp and disappeared through a doorway.

"Shem, brother of Japheth, what have you done? Everyone is talking nonsense."

"Bakta. Praise Yahweh! I understand what you are saying."

"Yes, but my workers do not." Bakta spread his arms out and gestured. "All my workers have abandoned their work. I cannot understand anyone."

Shem pointed up. "I met with Nimrod at the top. You were right. He would not listen, and would have hurt me, but Yahweh intervened. If you have family, go get them and meet me as quickly as you can at Eber and Lebana's dwelling. I think Yahweh would like us to know each other better. Lebana is the woman with child who helps the women cook."

Bakta nodded. "I know their dwelling."

Shem started off for Eber's and then shouted back at Bakta. "Bring supplies for a journey and bring with you anyone who understands your words. May Yahweh keep you safe."

**

Lebana paced back and forth next to the eating table. "I hope nothing bad has happened to Eber."

Jazel took Lebana's hand. "Come sit with me. I am sure Eber will be back soon."

A knock sounded on the door. Shem sprang to open it. Bakta stood glancing behind him.

"Bakta, come in."

Bakta entered along with another woman, and the young woman, Avala. Before Shem could close the door, a hand from outside grabbed the door and held it open.

"Eber," Shem exclaimed and then looked out the door. "You are alone?"

Eber slowly nodded.

Lebana jumped up from her stool and hurried as quickly as a woman with child could to the door. She hugged her husband hard.

Eber looked at Shem and shook his head. "None of our friends understood me."

Lebana pushed away from the hug. "Mereb and Onam? Rinna and Seba?"

Eber shook his head.

Lebana pressed her head against Eber's chest and cried.

Shem looked at Avala. "Bakta, I thought she did not..."

"She is my daughter. She was overwhelmed and wanted to run home to her mother. I was afraid to let her go by herself." He put his arm on the other woman's shoulder. "This is my wife, Hanoch.

Shem allowed a short time for greeting one another and then grabbed a stool and said, "Come and sit down. It is time I explain what has happened and why."

Everyone took stools, scooted them to the table, and sat.

Shem scanned the faces around the table. Jazel placed herself next to Shem and smiled back at him.

Shem cleared his throat. "When my family left the Ark to begin our new lives at the foot of the great mountain, Yahweh told us to spread throughout the land and cover the earth. My father and Japheth's family traveled east. My brother, Ham, and his family traveled to the southern lands. Jazel and I came across the plain to an area not far from here."

Lebana leaned against Eber and dried her eyes on his shoulder.

"Nimrod's plans were in defiance against Yahweh's commands. He was building a great tower to attract people to one place, where he, not Yahweh, could rule over them. I confronted him but he would not listen, so Yahweh intervened and confused everyone's speech. Yahweh is now using this confusion to scatter his people. But, because we all still understand each other, I believe he has selected us to be together."

Avala tightly hugged Bakta's arm while he and Hanock held hands on the table.

"This city is no longer safe. We should leave and go to my village where we should find others whose speech we understand."

"We have half a day before nightfall to distance us from all this confusion and fear, and then four or five days to get to know each other better before reaching our village. I do not know what to expect when we arrive, but I know Yahweh will work it out."

Shem paused to allow the families to talk it over.

Jazel took an urn and a cup from the table and motioned for Shem to follow her into the food preparation room. She filled the cup and handed it to him.

"Thanks."

He smiled and then drank it all down. She lay her head against his shoulder and he wrapped his arm around her. When the other room became silent, they returned and sat the table.

Eber glanced at his wife and then spoke. "Lebana and I would like to know more about Yahweh and his plans. And I would like my child to know his family. We are ready to join you."

Bakta laughed. "I have no one to give orders to anymore. And Avala would like to know more about the Ark and all the animals. We will join you as well."

Shem slapped both hands on the table and stood. "Then it is settled. Collect the supplies you want to travel with. I think there will be more than you need once we get to my village."

***

Very few people walked the streets. Shem called out to those they saw, hoping to find anyone else who understood them, but everyone responded by running away. The large gates lay open. No spearmen in sight.

Shem and his new family quietly passed through and followed the stone road past the empty merchant booths. What used to be a lively sea of tents with children playing and the sound of laughter, now was a silent hodge-podge of mangled fabrics and broken tent poles laying strewn across the area.

No one spoke again until the landscape finally blocked their view of the city and the tower.

Shem put his arm around Jazel. "I am glad I convinced you to come with me on this trip."

Jazel pushed away from him. "You…convinced me?" She punched his shoulder, and then leaned in and hugged him.

Chapter 22

(Approximately 370 years later.)

"Naked we came into the world and naked we leave. Blessed be the name of Yahweh." Shem watched as dirt was raked back into the grave over the body.

How many times had he, as the Elder, pronounced those words at a funeral? Too many times. He understood that it came with the position. Most villages had an elder that officiated at funerals. It seemed right to the people and for the people, but it no longer seemed right to Shem.

That night, after the evening meal, Shem took the short walk to the edge of the bluff. He sat on a bench overlooking the mouth of the Tigris as it slipped into the sea. The moon illuminated the tips of the waves as the fresh water from the Tigris met the saltwater from the sea.

Even with the beauty of this view, he still missed his view of the the mountain holding the ark. He knew that long ago the smoke plume he had viewed from his home across the plain had disappeared and snow now replaced it, but in his mind, he could still see it and long for it. He also knew why they left their home and journeyed east across the plains to this place.

Nimrod.

Sometime after the division of languages at the tower, Nimrod traveled west, and built the great city, Nineveh, not too far from their village. Evil attracts evil, Shem discovered. He wanted no part of it. Eber and Bakta along with many families from the village felt the same and came east with him, feeling more comfortable putting further space between them and Nimrod.

The path to the bluff overlooking the Tigris showed the ware of many years of use. Shem sat and fingered the rough end of the wooden armrest next to him. He had just built this bench to replace the older worn out bench that replaced the first bench he built. Would he eventually ware this one as smooth as the others?

A light approached from behind. Jazel, carrying a torch, shoved one end of it into the sandy soil and sat next to him.

She snuggled close. "This bench is not as smooth as the other one."

He put an arm over her shoulder.

"You were very quiet tonight. Is something wrong?"

He fidgeted. "It was the funeral."

"You have spoken at countless funerals. What was different about this one?'

"Nothing," he said. "That is the problem. All funerals are the same."

Jazel lifted her head from his shoulder. "You are not making sense."

He raised his arm from her shoulder, stood, and faced her. "No, it is the funerals that make no sense. Many years ago, we buried our children, Arphaxad, Elam, Ashur, Lud, Aram, and all the others. Then, we buried their children. We even buried Eber's children and grand-children." He started pacing in front of the bench. "Except for Eber, we continue to bury our descendants born hundreds of years after the flood." His voice began to rise. "It should be the other way around. They should be officiating at our funerals."

"Shem, calm down." She grabbed his hand. "Sit back down with me."

Shem knelt, took her hand, and put it in front of her face. "Jazel, look at your hand. Look at my hand. Even in the dim torch light, you can see they look the same as when we built the ark. Have you seen the hands, the faces, the bodies of the people we bury? They are old and wrinkled, bent from age like the benches I replaced. This is not right."

She pulled her hand from his. "Do you think I have not been aware of this a long time? The women come to me and ask what my secret is that keeps me looking young.

Tears ran down her cheeks. "I cannot answer them. Many do not want to be my friend after they age, and I remain the same."

He leaned forward and held her tight.

Jazel wept. "Shem...why are we the only ones not aging? What is Yahweh...doing to us?"

"I think the question should be; What is Yahweh doing to his people? Before the flood we would be considered normal. If Japheth and Ham still lived close, we could be sure, but, for some reason, Yahweh has determined a shorter life span for people born after the flood.

***

Shem lay in bed, his mind swirled with questions. Why is Yahweh shortening the lives of his people? If he still loved his people would he not give them long lives? What about people like Nimrod? And cities like Babylon and Nineveh? They seem to be thriving.

Shem had heard the stories about the evil people of Sodom and Gomorrah in the lands to the west, and how Yahweh rained fire and brimstone down from the sky and destroyed them. Why did he not do the same to these cities?

It seems people have become as evil as before the flood. How long before there is no place to go to get away from them? Did Yahweh flood the world in vane? What was the point if nothing has changed?

What about the jewel from his grandfather's dream? Could it be the First Man was wrong? Does Yahweh really love them enough to remove the evil from their hearts and restore them to intimacy with him forever?

Suddenly, Shem was standing in front of the ark on top of the mountain. All the animals were gone. His father appeared in front of him holding a small lamb with a jeweled pendant hanging from its neck.

"Here," he said, as he handed Shem the lamb. "This is for the sacrifice."

Shem took the lamb with the jeweled pendant. It was spotless, perfect to use as a sacrifice. His father disappeared and Shem's son, Arphaxad, now stood facing him in front of their dwelling on the plain.

Shem gave the lamb with the jeweled pendant to his son. "Here. Take this lamb for the sacrifice."

His son, Arphaxad, took the lamb, but many people passed between them and Shem could not see what happened to the lamb. He then glimpsed Eber giving the spotless lamb with the jeweled pendant to his son, Peleg, telling him the same thing. More people came between them and Shem lost Peleg in the crowd.

Panic welled up inside Shem.

What happened to the lamb? His body ached to know. He searched and searched, but, could not find it. Just as he was about to despair, a large scroll rolled against his leg. He picked it up and unrolled it.

It was a map of the surrounding lands.

A figure of a spotless lamb wearing a jeweled pendant emerged over Chaldea, hovering over the city of Ur. The lamb slowly moved west across the plain of Shinar and stopped in an area called Paddan Aram.

Shem awoke and quickly sat up in bed breathing hard. "Paddan Aram."

Jazel stirred beside him. "Did you say something?

"We must go to Paddan Aram."

With eyes still closed, she patted the empty space next to her. "Go back to sleep."

Shem lay his head back onto the bed and stared at the dark ceiling. He could feel his heart beating. Yahweh had shown him a vision. What did it mean? He knew sleep was no longer possible. He rolled slowly out of bed and tip-toed to the table in the eating room. What could he do until the sun rose?

Chapter 23

Jazel stopped as the road crested a small rise and scanned the next valley. "This ground is rocky. It is much better for grazing sheep than growing vegetables. Do you really think we are going to find the answer to our questions in Paddan Aram?"

"I hope so." Shem stood next to her and followed her gaze. "If we do not, we have walked a long way for nothing. The dream was very vivid and showed specifically the sacrificial lamb stopping there."

Jazel continued walking. "I still do not know what the lamb has to do with the jewel."

Shem paused, watching a hawk, with wings stretched, hovering motionless in the sky against the wind.

"We know the jewel represents Yahweh's loving commitment to find a way to remove our sinfulness from us and restore us to an intimate relationship with him for all time?"

Jazel turned and faced Shem. "Then why did he say the lamb was for the sacrifice? What sacrifice? It does not make sense to me."

"Yahweh would not have given me the dream with the map if he did not want us to follow it." Shem continued to scan the valley as he started his descent. "We should be getting close."

They walked until the sun was past midway and came to a well with flocks of sheep grazing nearby. Two young men ambled up to the well and rolled a large stone away to allow the water to flow to an area where the sheep could drink.

Shem called out to them. "Whose sheep are these?"

One of them called back. "They are my father's sheep. We bring them here from the pasture to water them each day."

Shem stepped closer. "My wife and I are travelers from Ur across the plain. Would your father welcome a couple guests for the night?"

The older of the two rubbed his well-trimmed beard. "My father's grandfather came from Ur. I am sure he would enjoy sharing a meal with you."

Shem bowed. "May Yahweh bless you and your family."

Jazel reached back and pulled her head scarf up over her hair.

The two young shepherds conferred briefly and then the younger one stepped forward. "I am Judah. I will take you to my father. My brother, Simeon, will take the sheep back to the pasture. My father also follows the ways of Yahweh."

"It pleases me to hear that. I am Shem. We will follow you to your father."

The three of them followed a path across another pasture and through a grove of trees. They came to a group of tent structures. Several women watched them approach from an outdoor cooking area off to the side. A large table surrounded by many stools spanned the distance between the cooking area and the tents. A young girl played with a small boy chasing him around the stools. Beyond that, laundry hung drying on cords.

To the other side, a small fenced area kept young lambs from wandering. It looked like these people had lived there for a while. Several chickens came toward them as they approached the tents. Judah shewed them away.

"Father!" Judah shouted from the tent opening. "We have visitors."

Judah entered the tent briefly and reappeared followed by a man in a tunic. His beard covered a wide smile. His eyes sparkled under bushy brows.

Shem bowed his head. "I am Shem. May Yahweh bless you for your kindness."

"I am Jacob." He returned a slight bow. "My son tells me you are from Ur and follow Yahweh." He looked back and forth between the two. "We have not had any visitors from Ur. And, other than my family, there are none that follow Yahweh here. We will have much to talk about."

"None following Yahweh in all of Paddan Aram?" Shem asked.

"Only my family, here in Paddan Aram, and in the whole land of Canaan beyond this, only my father and brother."

Shem thought back to the time after the flood when his father cursed Canaan for Ham's disrespect of him. *And now the land of Canaan shows no respect for Yahweh.*

"My sons should be returning from their labors soon and then we will share a meal together. Judah, take Shem's wife to Rachel and the other women." He bowed his head to Jazel. "My wives will enjoy your company."

Wives? Shem caught Jazel's eyes.

Jazel winked at Shem as Judah led her away.

"Come," Jacob pulled the tent flap open. "relax from your journey. You are a long way from Ur."

Shem followed Jacob inside to a carpeted area with many pillows, cushions of various sizes, and wool blankets strewn around a knee-high table in the middle. Jacob gestured and Shem made himself comfortable.

A woman appeared and set an urn and two cups on the table.

Jacob filled the two cups and handed one to Shem. "No better wine than what comes from the grapes grown on these hills."

Shem took the cup. "To your health, Jacob. Yahweh be praised."

They both sipped.

"Tell me, Shem." Jacob's eyes seemed like they could see right through him. "Why are you traveling so far from Ur?"

Shem felt those eyes were searching him for the answer. "I am following a dream Yahweh gave me."

"A dream?" Jacob refilled his cup.

Shem did not feel comfortable explaining a dream he, himself, did not understand, so he tried to change the subject. "Your other son, Simeon, told us your grandfather came from Ur. Why did he leave his family and come all the way to this country?"

Jacob chugged another drink. "That is a good question. I do not tell the people here about it because they would not understand, but I will tell you because I think you will."

Jacob leaned into the pillows. "Yahweh came to my grandfather, Abram, and told him to leave his family and go to a distant land. He said he would bless him with descendants as many as the sands of the sea.

"And that all the nations of the earth would be blessed through him. Yahweh even changed his name to Abraham, father of many."

"That is quite a blessing."

Jacob lowered his eyes. "Yes, and my grandfather had much faith. More than me."

"How is that?"

"At that time, my grandfather had only one son, the only son through whom the promise of Yahweh could be fulfilled. Yahweh told him to build an altar and sacrifice his son on the altar. He bound his only son, my father, and raised his knife to slay him, but Yahweh stayed his hand and provided a ram to sacrifice instead. After that he always said, 'Yahweh will provide the sacrifice.'"

Hmmm, Yahweh will provide the sacrifice. Shem thought of his dream and the lamb with the jewel that was passed from father to son for the sacrifice.

"My grandfather had much faith, but he died not seeing the fulfillment of Yahweh's promise."

Shem shrugged. "I have noticed that Yahweh's timing is much slower than our timing."

Jacob refilled Shem's cup. "Yahweh also went to my father, and later, to me and reaffirmed the promise made to my grandfather, telling us each that the whole land of Canaan would be ours, and that the whole world would be blessed through us."

He sighed. "And yet, here I am, with my eleven sons and a daughter, in Paddan Aram, working as a hired hand."

Shem set his cup down and leaned forward. "And you are doubting Yahweh's promise?"

Jacob slowly shook his head. "It is hard to see how the promise could come to fulfillment."

Shem stared at Jacob, who looked like a man in need of a drink of fresh water. He now understood why Yahweh brought him here.

"Jacob. Listen to me." He spoke even and direct. "I too doubted a promise Yahweh made to my grandfather, and to my father. I also did not see how it could come to pass."

Jacob lifted his head. "You also?"

"After many years, my grandfather died without seeing the fulfillment, as yours has. But then, Yahweh did the impossible. He performed a miracle. A miracle so big, nothing like it has ever been seen before. And after listening to you, I believe he is not yet done performing miracles. I believe Yahweh has plans to bless the people he created and has brought me all the way from Ur to encourage you to not give up on what he promised."

Jacob stood, walked to the tent entrance, and stared up at the sky.

"Maybe I have become too comfortable here in Paddan Aram. Maybe it is time to return to Canaan and see what miracle Yahweh has in store to fulfill his promise. Thank you, Shem for your words."

Jacob waved to someone outside. "My sons have returned. The women have prepared us a meal. Let us join them at the table outside." Jacob's eyes sparkled again. "It is time to eat and laugh and share stories."

Chapter 24

Shem and Jazel reached the top of the hill again and looked back at the valley of Paddan Aram.

Jazel put her arm around Shem's and squeezed. "Tell me what we learned from walking across this long hot plain of Shinar."

"I learned…that a man can have two wives."

Jazel dropped his arm and raised her fist.

Shem quickly put a hand in front of his shoulder. "Wait. Maybe I learned…that one wife is better than two."

Jazel laughed. "It took you all these years to learn that?"

As they continued walking, Shem tried again. "I learned that Yahweh has been making promises for a long time to people we knew nothing about. Promises to bless the nations of the world."

Jazel stopped and gazed across the open plain. "I have heard that since the confusion of languages, many nations of strange tongues have formed. In what way do you think Yahweh could bless these nations through Jacob's family? I do not think Jacob has any idea."

Shem thought briefly. "The lamb wearing the jewel in my dream stopped at Paddan Aram, so I know Jacob's family is associated with it. Jacob mentioned that Abraham's father's name was Terah. I remember a descendent of Eber named Terah living in Ur."

Jazel nodded. "Was not he the one that told everyone Yahweh had called him to go to the land of Canaan? He just took his family and disappeared."

"Jacob, according to my dream, must be a descendent of Eber and has been passed the sacrificial lamb with the jewel." Shem's smile dropped from his face. "But what is the sacrificial lamb for?"

They both walked a little further. Then Shem remembered his conversation with Jacob.

"Yahweh will provide!" he proclaimed.

"What?"

"Jacob told me that when Abraham went to the mountain to sacrifice his son, Isaac, Yahweh provided a ram caught in a thicket to be used for the sacrifice instead. He then named the place, 'Yahweh Will Provide.'

"He did not say, 'Yahweh Has Provided', because he was not looking back at what just happened, but ahead to a future time when Yahweh will again provide for a sacrifice."

Jazel put her hands against Shem's chest. "So, you think the lamb wearing the jewel represents a lamb that Yahweh will use as a special sacrifice?"

Shem took her hands from his chest and pushed her back slightly. "But how can sacrificing a lamb take away the sinful nature of everyone in the world? All this seems so confusing."

Jazel shoved his arms away, reached up, and caressed his cheeks with both hands. "You did not know how Yahweh was going to provide enough water to cover the whole world, but he did. You built the ark in faith not knowing how Yahweh would do it. Maybe by faith Yahweh will provide what we do not understand."

Shem stared into Jazel's eyes. A feeling came over him that he immediately understood.

The birds hushed and the air became still. A voice came to them from out of the air near them.

"My children, you labor for knowledge that is beyond you. Jazel is right. The answer is by faith. Faith in me. Know that I love you and have not abandoned you.

"I will take the family of Jacob to the land of Ham and forge them into a great nation. I will teach them my ways.

"Through a descendent of Jacob, I will show the world my love by providing him as a sacrificial lamb that will take away the sins of the world, by faith in me. I will restore my people to myself because I love them.

"Go home now and be at peace. You will be gathered to your ancestors after a full and rewarding life. Eber will close your eyes and speak words over you. I am Yahweh, who speaks, and it comes to pass."

Shem and Jazel fell to the ground and cried. Shem could not express his happiness and knew he did not have to. They hugged a long time before they helped each other up.

Shem turned and gazed back toward Paddan Aram. "I feel a peace that I have not felt for a long time."

"Because of Yahweh?"

"Because I now am assured, as my grandfather and the First Man were, that Yahweh's love for us is greater than the evil that separates us from him. He will... he *is* providing a way...a sacrifice so great, it will bring us into an intimacy with him we have never known."

Shem put his arm around Jazel's shoulder. "Did I ever tell you that Yahweh loves you?"

She laughed. "Did I ever tell you that Yahweh said I was right?"

Shem cringed. "Why do I have a feeling you are never going to let me forget."

"I know how forgetful you are." She poked him in his ribs. "You may need to be reminded occasionally."

He shook his head and they started walking. "It is going to be a long walk home."

Epilogue

Eber paused as he gazed at the crowd assembled in front of him. He recognized many family and friends from villages in the area. Many faces, though, he had never seen before. Probably brought here by their curiosity about the man lying before him.

My friend, you lived among us quietly and unassuming. You were qualified to be our leader, yet in most ways, you humbly served us, counseling us as a father might, always encouraging us in our relationship with Yahweh.

Who would we turn to now? Who will be a reminder to them…to me, that Yahweh loves us? What can I tell them? I did not personally see the wrath of Yahweh's flood. I did not experience his love in the safety of an ark filled with animals. I have no dreams from Yahweh, no stories from the beginning to assure me of Yahweh's love. I have only…had only…my friendship with you.

I will speak words over you, my friend, and commend you to Yahweh. I will then trust in your faith that someday a "special sacrifice" will be provided to rescue us from our sinful state, as you were rescued from the Flood.

Eber raised his arms high and the crowd became silent.

"People, we are here to honor the man, Shem. Let me tell you about this true hero of old."

Biblical Record of Shem's Ancestors

Two years after the flood, when Shem was 100 years old, he became the father of Arphaxad. After he became the father of Arphaxad, Shem lived 500 years and had other sons and daughters.

When Arphaxad had lived 35 years, he became the father of Shelah. And after he became the father of Shelah, Arphaxad lived 403 years and had other sons and daughters.

When Shelah had lived 30 years, he became the father of Eber. And after he became the father of Eber, Shelah lived 403 years and had other sons and daughters.

When Eber had lived 34 years, he became the father of Peleg. And after he became the father of Peleg, Eber lived 430 years and had other sons and daughters.

When Peleg had lived 30 years, he became the father of Reu. And after he became the father of Reu, Peleg lived 209 years and had other sons and daughters.

When Reu had lived 32 years, he became the father of Serug. And after he became the father of Serug, Rue lived 207 years and had other son and daughters.

When Serug had lived 30 years, he became the father of Nahor. And after he became the father of Nahor, Serug had other sons and daughters.

When Nahor had lived 29 years, he became the father of Terah. And after Terah became the father of Terah, Nahor lived 119 years and had other sons and daughters.

After Terah had lived 70 years, he became the father of Abram. Terah lived 205 years, and he died in Haran.

Abraham was 100 years old when his son, Isaac was born to him. Abraham lived 175 years.

Isaac was 66 years old when Rebekah gave birth to Jacob. Isaac lived 180 years.

Jacob lived in Egypt 17 years and the years of his life were 147.

This ancestral record from the Bible is more easily understood when transferred to a column bar graph.

Approximate Timeline from Shem to Jacob

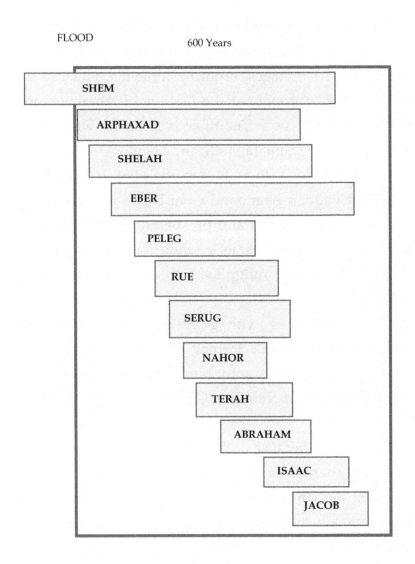

A Note from the Author

The Bible says Shem lived 500 years after the flood. We know that he was alive at the time of the Tower of Babel and the confusion of languages. From the timeline, you can see that he also lived throughout the lifetime of Abraham, and most of Isaac and Jacob's. The Bible is silent on what really happened to Noah, Shem, Japheth, and Ham.

The Bible does, though, record what happened to Jacob. He left Padden Aram and went back to Canaan. God changed his name to Israel and prospered his family. Later, his son, Joseph brought Israel's whole family into Egypt, where, after time, they multiplied into a vast people group called Hebrews.

God used Moses, with great miracles, to bring the Hebrews out of Egypt. He formed them into a nation and called them to be holy unto him. They conquered and inhabited all of Canaan, fulfilling God's promise to Abraham, Isaac, and Jacob.

Eventually, because of the sinfulness of God's people, God removed them from the "Promised Land" and scattered them among the surrounding nations. Only a remnant was allowed to remain, eventually becoming subject to the Roman Empire.

The sinful nature in man though, was still a problem.

It even separated God's holy people from him. This was what Shem observed from his unique perspective of living before and after the flood.

The judgment of the flood killed all but eight people in the whole world. And yet, only after a few generations, Shem heard about Sodom and Gomorrah, and could see the evil in Nimrod and the building of the Tower of Babel.

After 500 years, even though Shem could not see any change in the people, he was assured that God would still work another miracle to reconcile mankind to himself.

And God did.

To that small remnant in Judea, God sent his Son, Jesus, sinless in nature, a perfect sacrificial lamb, to die on the cross for the sins of the world.

It was a physical act with spiritual consequences. Because Jesus was, in essence, God, his shed blood and death was adequate payment for the penalty of all of mankind's sin, past, present, and future.

God created a new path to bring mankind back to him, a path that required faith in what Jesus did, and the humility to admit the personal need for it. Man's personal efforts to become righteous had failed to make even one righteous after 4000 years.

It was the miracle Shem knew was coming.

A miracle greater than flooding the world.

The flood brought judgment.

The cross brought mercy and grace.

Because of Adam's act of sin, many died. Because of Jesus' act of obedience, many are made alive forever.

May you become one of the many made alive through faith in Jesus.

Don Towle

Other Books by this Author

Lamech – A Man for God's Plans

Book 1 of the Heroes of Old Trilogy

A novel about Noah's father and the First Man

Enoch – He Walked with God

Book 2 of the Heroes of Old Trilogy

A novel about how Enoch became a prophet of God

Life – What is the Meaning?

Postulates the answer to the question:

Why were we created?

He Who Has Ears to Hear

A Unique View of End Times

Through Biblical Similes and Metaphors

I Want to be Left Behind

A Rebuttal of the End Times Doctrine

From the Popular Book Series